Surfer Girls

Bill Denton

ISBN: 0983653933
ISBN-13: 978-0-9836539-3-6

Published by Panoptic Books, an imprint of Assent Publishing

This book is a work of fiction. Names, characters, places, and incidents are products of this author's imagination or are used fictitiously. Any resemblance to actual events or locales or persons living or dead is entirely coincidental.

Welcome to New Tipton

New Tipton is a small city with a big secret. Something terrible happened there over 150 years ago, and the people of the city have paid a price ever since. In return for keeping the city's secrets, the residents of New Tipton have enjoyed enormous prosperity. Eventually the story behind the secret is discovered. With the secret revealed, what will happen to the city and its people?

Fortune Cookies

If you've ever seen a picture from days gone by of an old Chinese man, you know what Chang looks like. But that is about the only thing you will ever know about him. You'll never know about the secrets Chang carries in his head, or the ancient knowledge woven into the embroidery of the ageless silk robe he wears. You might get to taste one of his fortune cookies. If you do, you'd better hope you are deserving of only good fortune.

CHAPTER 1

As with many other things in life, it was all a matter of perspective. Most of the citizens of Delta City, Arkansas would describe this particular point in time as late in the day. But the Surfer Girls had often made their own rules, and for them, before six p.m. was day, while after six p.m. was night.

Even though it would be a couple of hours before the sun even began to think about setting in the middle of June, as the Surfer Girls sat on the patio drinking margaritas and trying to keep their conversation light, it was Tuesday night.

The three women talked about the things they'd seen in the stores, a recent season finale on TV, and some local gossip. But despite their best efforts, when they hit their third pitcher, they got to the subject they would really have preferred to stay away from.

There was simply no way for them to avoid discussing the body of the dead man that was lying in repose in Cairn's freezer.

CHAPTER 2

Delta City is hardly the sort of place where you would think to find a trio of forty-something women who go by the name of "Surfer Girls".

There is a lot of water around Delta City, ranging from the Mississippi River down to dinky little farm ponds, but the closest thing to a wave you'd ever find there was when one of the good old boys had one too many and fell out of his fishing boat with a splash. Needless to say, surfing was not one of the major activities in Delta City.

In truth, about the only major activity in Delta City was agriculture, and from those agrarian roots sprang Nicole Pauline Bailey on July 2, 1965.

Her mother, Merlene Bailey, was a wife. She kept house, cooked, and raised Nicole to be a wife, just as her own mother had done for her.

Nicole's father was Ray Dean Bailey, Sr., who owned enough prime farmland to qualify for the "planter" title even though he preferred "farmer". When he was in the midst of negotiating some sort of business deal, he frequently proclaimed that he was "just a plain old dirt farmer that don't know nothing about nothing but raising crops". This usually meant that whomever he was negotiating with left with a lot less money than he came with.

Nicole's brother, Ray Dean, Jr., was seventeen when she was born. He really liked the age difference because it gave him a baby sister to look up to him, while enabling him to avoid most of the responsibilities that fall on big brothers closer in age.

Planter or farmer or just dumb old country boy, Ray Dean Bailey, Sr. was the richest man in Delta City. And that meant that Nicole Bailey grew up as the most pampered and spoiled child in town.

One week to the day after the birth of Nicole, Barbara Ann Mason became the newest resident of Delta City. She was the daughter of Tom, the president of the Delta City Savings Bank, and Katherine, an English professor at Delta City University. Thanks to a long-term friendship that resulting in Ray Dean Bailey Sr. doing a lot of business with his bank, Tom Mason was the second richest man in Delta City.

As two young girls in a small town, whose parents were friends, and who lived only a couple of blocks from each other, it was natural that Nicole and Barbara would spend some of their earlier years playing together. When they started kindergarten, the nexus of what would become the Surfer Girls was formed.

CHAPTER 3

It was only ten minutes into Nicole and Barbara's first day of kindergarten, and already Nicole had taken command of every toy in the classroom, refusing to allow any of the other children to play with them.

Mrs. Jameson, the teacher, was well aware of two things. Since there was an active grapevine in Delta City, she already knew that Nicole was very much a spoiled brat. And in her 20 years of teaching, she had learned that if adults just stayed out of these kinds of situations the kids could usually work it out on their own, while often learning a lesson about getting along with others. She just stayed behind her desk and watched.

Among the toys Nicole had hoarded was a large shiny red fire engine. A little boy named Jake, whose father was a member of the volunteer fire department, had been eyeing it since he first came into the classroom.

The other kids had grouped up about 10 feet from Nicole, and Jake eased away from the group and began moving toward the fire truck. Nicole was watching him like a rattlesnake would watch its prey, and the minute he touched the fire truck she screamed, "I'm in charge of the toys, and you can't play with any of them!"

As Jake retreated to the group of kids, Mrs. Jameson smiled and thought "*Act 1.*"

None of the kids moved for about a minute. Then Barbara gave a disgusted sigh, walked over to right in front of Nicole, and picked up a toy Volkswagen beetle, painted to look like a ladybug.

Nicole immediately screamed, "I said nobody could play with the toys!"

Barbara just stared at her for a moment, then turned and walked over to a desk, where she sat down and began playing with the car.

Emboldened by Barbara's actions, Jake walked back over and picked up the fire engine. As Nicole screamed, "You can't play with that!" he walked over to the desk where Barbara was sitting, and the two were soon absorbed in a game of "chase" with the toy vehicles.

Her power trip shattered, Nicole began to sob as other kids came over and began picking out toys to play with.

Even though most of the other kids had toys, Nicole noticed that a few children did not. She looked at the kids without toys, and then focused on a girl, smaller than the other children, who seemed to be a bit withdrawn.

From the pile of untaken toys, Nicole withdrew a Raggedy Ann doll and walked over to the little girl. As she extended the toy, Nicole said, "If you'll be my friend I'll let you play with this doll."

The girl took the proffered doll, but sat with her head down as Nicole began babbling about little girl things.

Mrs. Jameson watched this with annoyance, and made a mental note to talk to Mrs. Bailey about the Nicole's attempt to buy a friend.

When the kids went outside for recess, Nicole immediately walked up to Barbara and said, "I thought you were my friend."

"No, my daddy is friends with your daddy and my mommy makes me play with you."

Nicole briefly looked hurt. Then she smiled and said almost plaintively, "Barbara, will you be my friend?"

"I'll think about it. But for now we can still play together."

Now, more than 30 years later, the relationship between Nicole and Barbara was such that they still played together, but where the issue of their friendship remained unresolved.

CHAPTER 4

The third member of the Surfer Girls entered the world quite a bit closer to the ocean than the other two, albeit the wrong ocean. On August 14, 1965, Karen Lynn Dumont was born to Randy and Lynn Dumont in Waltham, Massachusetts, a little over 10 miles from the Atlantic.

Randy had a degree in Textile Engineering from MIT, and when Karen was midway through the ninth grade, he moved his family to Delta City, where he would be managing a complex of three carpet mills. Lynn Dumont had a degree in Graphic Arts from Boston University and was an accomplished painter. But, following the birth of her daughter, Lynn spent the rest of her life doing what could only be described as "fading". Most of the time she could function on some level or another, but she gave an overall impression of not being quite there, and was eventually diagnosed as suffering from bipolar disorder and crushing depression.

A short time after the Dumont's move to Delta City, Karen became the third Surfer Girl, and a few months later, she became "Cairn".

.

CHAPTER 5

In addition to Karen Dumont, there was another new face at Delta City High School that semester, that of Donnie Taylor.

His parents had recently divorced, and Donnie and his mother had returned to her home state of Arkansas. After a short time in Pine Bluff, they moved to Delta City, where Donnie's mother worked for her brother in his TV repair shop.

Donnie was in line behind Karen Dumont the day they both enrolled at Delta City High School.

Donnie thought Karen was beautiful. When he met the other Surfer Girls, he thought they were beautiful, too. He spent a great deal of the rest of his life staring at some or all of the Surfer Girls, while the Surfer Girls never saw Donnie at all.

CHAPTER 6

Friday afternoon, Barbara was finally able to relax a little bit as she drank strawberry daiquiris with the other Surfer Girls. Sitting at the picnic table in her back yard, she thought, "*Nicole may be the leader of the Surfer Girls, but as usual it's me who keeps our asses out of a sling!*"

Barbara had spent the previous week making sure that Nicole kept her mouth shut and comforting Cairn to keep her from falling apart. She had guided the Surfer Girls through their normal activities, making sure that no one in Delta City would suspect them of doing anything wrong.

The dead man's body was still in Cairn's freezer. The Surfer Girls had managed to avoid any discussion of the subject since Tuesday, and it seemed that nobody else in Delta City was talking about it either.

There had been no house-to-house sweep by the Delta City Police Department. No one had called in the Arkansas State Police to help look for the missing man. No television crews had come down from Little Rock to do a report on the search.

The closest thing to a mention had been in yesterday's Delta City Journal, which Nicole was now reading aloud. "The headline says, 'Stolen Mercedes Found in Delta City'. Then it says 'Chief Harry Laird of the Delta City Police Department reported that a Mercedes convertible, which had been stolen in Dallas, was found in the parking lot of the University Club on Tuesday morning. The alleged thief, a career criminal with multiple convictions, has not yet been located. The investigation is continuing.'"

Until the other Surfer Girls read the article in the Journal, only Cairn knew exactly how the dead body came to be in her freezer. Barbara had been able to piece part of the story together from what Cairn had told her the night the man died. Things Barbara knew about Cairn had filled some of the other holes in the story, and with what was in the newspaper, Barbara now had a good idea of what had happened.

CHAPTER 7

The dead man's journey to Cairn's freezer had begun the previous Monday evening. The Surfer Girls were sitting at their usual table at the University Club.

Barbara was fending off the attentions of a guy she semi-remembered from high school.

"C'mon, Barbara, go home with me tonight. I'm the only guy in here that you haven't been to bed with."

"No, Mikey, I'm going home by myself tonight. I've had a long weekend and I'm tired."

Mikey replied, "Tell ya what, I'll give you a nice back rub to help you relax and then we can fuck."

"Mikey, no!"

"Barbara, you've fucked every one of my friends, why won't you fuck me?"

Barbara gave him a hard look and said, "I fucked your friends because I thought they might be good in bed."

Barbara almost added, "*But I'm not going to fuck you because I don't think you would be worth a damn*," but a hard glance from Cairn stopped her. Instead, she just left the implication, and said, "Mikey, I really am tired. But you can ask me some other time."

As Mikey mumbled something and walked away, Barbara turned to Cairn and mouthed "Thanks!"

Cairn whispered, "I'm just trying to help you out. You know what can happen when you start cutting guys balls off like that!"

Barbara and Cairn both knew what could happen, and what once had happened. Cairn had seen the pictures of Barbara with a black eye and a cut lip. Nicole knew nothing about the incident that resulted in

Barbara's injuries, as it was one of many secrets that Barbara and Cairn didn't share with her.

Nicole turned toward the bar and yelled, "Could you bring us another round over here?"

Turning back to the other Surfer Girls she said, "Let's just drink this one and call it a night, okay?" Despite the fact that it would only be their third drink of the evening, both Barbara and Cairn nodded in assent.

"What a weekend," Barbara noted. Turning to Nicole she said, "I like going to Dallas, but do you even know what charity that ball was for?"

Nicole replied, "Of course I do! It's…it's…well, I guess all of these drinks are affecting my memory. I can look it up when I get home and call you."

Laughing inwardly, Barbara thought, "*Right. Two drinks and you can't remember the name of a charity, but you could have two hundred drinks and still manage to recite every slight you've ever suffered.*"

"That's okay, Nicole. I'm sure it was for a good cause. You're always attending these functions and doing good things for others." To herself, Barbara thought, "*Or at least your daddy's checkbook is.*" She marveled at how the people who ran those charity events could sniff out people with money, even if they lived in Delta City, Arkansas.

The Surfer Girls talked about this and that as they consumed their final drink. Normally, Monday night was the beginning of the Surfer Girl's ramp up toward the weekend, but the trip to Dallas had left them all tired. Though they tried to give the impression that, as usual, they were partying hard, they were really only going through the motions.

"Damn," Cairn said, as she put her empty glass on the table. The other women followed her eyes to a man standing at the bar alone. He was good looking in an average sort of way, and nicely dressed without being overly fashionable. Sipping his beer, he saw the Surfer Girls looking at him and gave them a pleasant smile.

Barbara asked, "Do you know him?"

"No," Cairn replied, "but looking at him is making me horny!"

Barbara said, "I thought we were going to leave after this drink."

Cairn replied, "Ya'll go ahead. I think I'll have another drink and see if I can get that guy in bed." Cairn looked toward the bartender and extended one finger, indicating that only she would be having another drink.

As Barbara and Nicole left, Cairn began to plot her strategy, trying to figure out a way to approach the man without being overly obvious.

She took a sip of her drink, and then muttered, "Damn." An attractive woman had come out of the ladies room and joined the man, and it was obvious that they were some type of couple.

Cairn quickly drained her glass and headed out the door. When she reached her car, a Mercedes convertible was pulling into the space next to hers. A man got out and asked, "Do they have cigarettes in this place?"

"Yeah, there's a machine just inside the front door."

She watched as the man walked toward the club. He had a rugged appearance, but the vehicle he was driving belied his blue-collar look. She thought, "*Oooh, that one might be fun,*" and mentally debated going back inside for another drink. However, before she could make a decision, she saw the man coming back toward her while ripping the cellophane off a cigarette package and lighting up.

"Just making a quick stop, huh?" Cairn inquired.

Extending the cigarette, the man replied, "Just taking care of my bad habit."

Coyly, Cairn asked, "Is that the only bad habit you have?"

"Well, I enjoy a little Jack Daniels from time to time, and when I've got a long drive ahead I usually have a little nose candy with me."

"*Run, run, run!*" the little voice screamed inside Cairn's head. White powder had been a big part of her year in Chicago, and she had sworn she'd never do it again. But horniness took over and she said, "Why don't you jump in my car and we'll run over to my house for a couple of drinks."

The man smiled and reached for the door handle.

As far as Cairn knew, nobody had seen her drive away with the man. No one else was in the parking lot, and no cars had passed by on the highway in front of the club.

She didn't know that Donnie Taylor was sitting in his car at Mike's Restaurant, across the highway. Donnie knew that the Surfer Girls would be at the University Club, and that they usually left early on Monday nights. He'd gotten a little late night snack, and was sitting in Mike's parking lot waiting for the Surfer Girls to appear.

He had stared intently when Nicole and Barbara came out, and was a bit surprised that Cairn wasn't with them. For the millionth time Donnie ran his eyes up and down the bodies of two of the women he loved. As Nicole and Barbara drove away, Donnie began gently stroking his cock through his jeans. He stopped when he saw what was happening in the University Club parking lot.

Donnie could see Cairn talking briefly to a man, who then walked into the club. Cairn was still standing in the parking lot, and Donnie undressed her with his eyes, just as he had mentally undressed Nicole and Barbara. When the man returned from the club, he had a short conversation with Cairn, and then he got into her car.

Seeing Cairn leave with the man mildly irritated Donnie. He knew that from time to time Cairn got a little crazy and picked up the first man in sight. Donnie had tried to figure out a pattern to her actions, and he took great pains to be near her when he thought she might be horny. As always, Cairn just looked right through him.

Donnie slowly drained the last of his milkshake. Aware that he would have no more opportunities to stare at any of the Surfer Girls outside the University Club, he started his car and pulled out of Mike's parking lot.

CHAPTER 8

Almost as soon as they got into Cairn's house, the man she had picked up at the University Club grabbed her, pulled her close, and kissed her hard.

"Perfect," she thought. *"No muss and no fuss, just get it on."*

On the drive to Cairn's house, there had been almost no conversation, no exchange of names. This would not be a night of intimacy and romance, just some hopefully good fucking. That would be that, and that was just fine with Cairn.

Still holding Cairn's arms, the man said, "As I recall, you promised me a drink."

"And as I recall, you said you like Jack." Leading the way toward the kitchen, she took down two glasses and a bottle of liquor.

"Straight?" she inquired, and he replied, "You got it!"

As she splashed the liquid into the glasses, the man sat down on a stool at the breakfast bar that separated the kitchen from the living room. He pulled out a paper package and poured some white powder onto the countertop. Cairn removed one of those fake credit cards from some junk mail and handed it to him, along with his drink.

After taking a sip of his drink, the man expertly turned the cocaine into two equal lines with the credit card. Taking a dollar bill from his pocket, he rolled it into a tube. Smiling, he extended it toward Cairn.

The little voice in Cairn's head was screaming *"No, no, no!"* as loud as it could. Ignoring it, she put the rolled up bill into her nostril and lowered her head toward the counter.

When Cairn raised her head, she felt that old familiar feeling that cocaine gave her, a feeling she had once loved, but one she had spent the last couple of decades trying to avoid experiencing again.

The man had his head down, and when he raised it, Cairn said, "Ohh…kay. I think we should go into the bedroom."

Turning off the lights in the kitchen and the living room, Cairn led the man down the hall. Entering the bedroom, she turned on the lights, said, "Excuse me for a minute," and walked toward the bathroom.

CHAPTER 9

Donnie couldn't resist driving by Cairn's house on his way home. He was sitting at the stop sign beside her house, waiting for an oncoming car to pass, and saw the lights in the front of her house go off and the bedroom lights come on.

As the oncoming car passed in front of him, Donnie waved to the driver, Dan Arthur Truman, one of Delta City's half-dozen police officers.

CHAPTER 10

Cairn hadn't really needed to use the bathroom. She had just wanted to give her body a second to become re-acclimated to the cocaine rushing through her system.

Coming back into the bedroom, she saw the man standing there naked with an almost evil smile on his face and his dick sticking straight out.

She smiled and walked toward him and began to lower herself to her knees, but before she reached the floor, he grabbed her hair, forced her down, and stuck his cock in her mouth.

"No, wait, slow down." Cairn was trying to say the words but couldn't do it with her mouth full of dick. She thought, "*This is rapidly becoming not fun.*"

Suddenly the cocaine paranoia kicked in, and she instinctively bit down on what was in her mouth.

The man screamed and leapt backwards, tripping over the clothes he had discarded on the floor. His forehead hit the edge of the dresser hard, and he fell limply to the floor.

CHAPTER 11

Nicole and Barbara arrived at Cairn's house shortly after her frantic phone call to Barbara and found Cairn sitting naked on the couch and staring off into space. Wordlessly, she pointed toward the bedroom.

Nicole could only stare at the man on the floor, but Barbara walked over to the body to check for a pulse. Cairn was now standing in the doorway, and Barbara looked at her and said, "He's dead."

There was a surreal quality to the scene. Three fortyish women, one of them naked, all staring at the nude body of the dead man on the bedroom floor.

Barbara asked, "Did you know him, Cairn?" Cairn gave a negative shake of her head.

Barbara continued, "So how did he get here?"

Cairn replied, "I picked him up in the parking lot of the University Club and brought him home."

Pointing to the pile of clothes on the floor, Barbara said, "Nicole, see if he has any ID."

Nicole quickly went through the man's jeans, finding nothing in the first three pockets, but in the final one, she found a large wad of money. As she was withdrawing the cash, a small paper bundle fell out and landed on the floor.

Picking it up, Nicole asked, "What's this?"

Barbara knew a few things about Cairn that Nicole didn't. She looked sharply at Cairn who just nodded and lowered her head.

In a commanding voice Barbara said, "Nicole, take it and flush it down the toilet."

"But what is it?" asked Nicole.

Barbara's voice was flat and cold as she ordered, "Nicole, just flush it!"

Nicole walked into the bathroom and flushed the paper bundle down the toilet, and when she returned, Barbara's tone was softer as she said, "Nicole, why don't you start some coffee? I think we may need it."

CHAPTER 12

Barbara had helped Cairn get into jeans and a tee shirt, and the Surfer Girls were sitting at the breakfast bar drinking coffee. Other than the fact that they would normally still be drinking alcohol at this hour and that there was a dead man in the next room it might have been two o'clock in the morning on any other day.

With her characteristic bluntness Barbara said, "Now let me get this straight, Cairn. You were gonna suck his dick but he tried to force you to do it so you bit his cock and he fell and hit his head and died. Is that pretty much it?"

Cairn nodded, and Nicole asked, "And that's when you called Barbara?"

Cairn answered, "Yeah, I just didn't know what else to do."

Nicole idly observed, "Cairn, when you step in it, you really step in it good!"

Barbara angrily interjected, "Shut up, Nicole! That's not helping anything." Continuing, she asked, "Anybody got any ideas?"

Cairn quietly said, "I'd love to cut off his dick and force-feed it to him."

Nicole laughed as Barbara dryly observed, "Given that he's dead I don't think that's an option."

Cairn said, "Well, what I'd really like to do is get that bastard out of my bedroom as soon as possible."

Again Nicole laughed, and said, "Remember how those Mafia guys hid that dead guy in a meat cooler on Law & Order that time? We could take this guy out to the meat packing plant and hide him behind some of those dead cows."

"We should probably call the cops," said Barbara.

Nicole added, "I saw Dan Arthur Truman on patrol earlier. He might could take care of things."

Cairn erupted, "Damn good idea, Nicole! We can get Dan Arthur over here and you can pull down your blouse and give him a little tit-shot like you used to do to get out of speeding tickets when we were in high school." Beginning to sob, she continued, "Goddamn it, this ain't a '55 in a 35 zone'. We're talking about a dead guy!"

Barbara had been quietly thinking, and said, "You know, Nicole might actually have the right idea. The first thing we really need to do is get the body out of Cairn's bedroom. After that, we can take a little time to figure out what to do next."

Barbara asked, "Cairn, have you still got that big old chest freezer in the shed out in your backyard?"

Cairn replied, "Yeah."

Barbara continued, "Is there anything in it other than that gallon of ice cream you put in there the day you bought the freezer?"

Cairn shook her head and said, "No."

Barbara said, "Okay, here's what we'll do. We'll put the body in the freezer. I don't think anybody will see us doing it this late at night. He didn't bleed any, so there's really nothing to clean up. Then we'll just go on about our business for a couple of days while we figure something else out."

Nicole said, "That's easy enough for you, Barbara! You went to nurse school so you're used to being around dead people. But I'm not going to touch any dead bodies, especially naked dead bodies!"

Barbara angrily replied, "Nicole, if you give me any crap I'll make you grab him by the dick and haul him out to the freezer all by yourself. Cairn's our friend. Now come on and help me."

Less than five minutes later Barbara closed the lid on the freezer with a resounding thump. Following Cairn's instructions, Nicole located the key on a shelf above the freezer and locked it, then turned to the others and said, "Well, that's that. Anyone want breakfast?"

CHAPTER 13

The following Friday afternoon, as the Surfer Girls sipped their strawberry daiquiris, they weren't the only people discussing the now-dead car thief.

In his office in the Delta City Municipal building, Police Chief Harry Laird was meeting with Dan Arthur Truman, the policeman who had been on duty the night that the thief had left the Mercedes in the University Club parking lot. Joining them were Lee Mitchell, the Arkansas State Police officer assigned to Delta City, and Michael Bell, the District Attorney, who had recently moved to Delta City from Little Rock.

Normally, the recovery of a stolen car would have merited little more than a brief passing-in-the-hallway chat between Dan Arthur and Chief Laird. However, this situation had turned out to be more than just an ordinary carjacking.

Lee Mitchell was speaking, "Okay, here's what's up, guys. Turns out that old boy who stole the Mercedes knocked the owner in the head while he was taking it, and the owner died yesterday so the Dallas cops would really like to get their hands on this guy."

Chief Laird asked, "Do we know anything about him, Lee?"

"We found some prints in the Mercedes and were able to ID him. His name was Terry Harding, and he's got a record a mile long in just about every state from Georgia to Nevada. Mostly armed robbery and drug stuff, but he also did a couple of rapes and there's a couple of dead bodies some other departments would like to talk to him about."

Chief Laird said, "It'd be quite a feather in our cap if we caught him so I'll make sure my guys go all out on this one."

Lee Mitchell said, "Thanks, Harry. Those Dallas cops sometimes think Arkansas cops ain't nothing but a bunch of rednecks!"

Chief Laird guffawed and said, "Well, the Delta City Police Department is a bunch of rednecks, and damn proud of it, but that sure as hell don't make us stupid."

Turning toward the other Delta City cop, he said, "Dan Arthur, you were on patrol the night before the Mercedes turned up. Did you see anything out of the ordinary, or were you off sleeping somewhere?"

"Hell no, I wasn't sleeping. The only thing that might be considered out of the ordinary was just Donnie Taylor sniffin' around after Cairn Dumont although it would be more out of the ordinary if he weren't following one of the Surfer Girls around."

The District Attorney asked, "Who's Donnie Taylor?"

Chief Laird replied, "Donnie owns Delta City Appliance World with his mama and ever since high school he's been trying to get next to the Surfer Girls. What was it you called him, Lee?"

"A benign stalker."

D.A. O'Malley said, "A stalker, huh. Is that anything we need to be doing something about?"

Dan Arthur replied, "Nah. All he does is follow the Surfer Girls around and gawk at them and I don't think it bothers them cause I don't think any of them even know he's there."

Everybody laughed, and Lee Mitchell asked, "Do you think you might could have a talk with Donnie, Dan Arthur, and see if maybe he saw anything?"

Grinning broadly, Dan Arthur said, "No problem. I'll just drive over by Nicole Bailey's house tonight and see if she still undresses with the shades open. If she does I'm sure Donnie will be around before the night is over."

CHAPTER 14

It was quite possible that Nicole would be undressing with the shades open tonight, if she didn't do something even worse. Even though she was worried, Barbara managed to smile at the other two Surfer Girls as she brought out a third pitcher of strawberry daiquiris.

While she was doing her best to make sure the Surfer Girls acted normal and kept a low profile, Barbara knew that it wouldn't be out of character for Nicole to take off her clothes on the town square before the night was over since she'd managed to do it at least once a year since her high school days. Somehow, Nicole seemed to have a knack for saying or doing exactly the wrong thing at exactly the wrong time.

Smiling to herself, Barbara thought, "*Only with Nicole would taking off your clothes on the town square be considered normal!*"

In a voice that was almost whining, Nicole asked, "Cairn, why'd you say that the other night about me pulling down my blouse and giving cops tit-shots? I never did that."

Barbara almost choked on her drink as she thought, "*Oh boy, here we go!*" But she couldn't resist laughing and saying, "Come on, Nicole. You know you've managed to show your tits to just about everybody in the State of Arkansas!"

Cairn also laughed and said, "Too bad your little adventure in L.A. didn't work out. You might have ended up with big enough boobs to get me out of killing a dozen guys!"

The "little adventure in L.A." had occurred in the summer of 1980, just before Nicole, Barbara, and Cairn started the tenth grade. It was the summer when Karen Dumont became Cairn, and when the three teenagers became the Surfer Girls.

Nicole laughed and said, "How was I supposed to know that plastic surgeon in Beverly Hills wouldn't give me a boob job because I was under age?"

Nicole had gone to Los Angeles ostensibly to spend a week with her cousin Maureen, but she also had another item on her agenda. While she had more money than anybody else in Delta City, had more stylish clothing than anybody else in Delta City, and had a nicer car than anybody else in Delta City, she did not have the largest breasts at Delta City High School. And for Nicole, that just would not do.

Maureen had told her that she wouldn't be able to get breast implants because of her age, but Nicole had petulantly replied, "With Daddy's money I can get anything I want!"

Unfortunately, "Daddy's money" didn't talk quite as loudly in Beverly Hills as it did in Delta City, so after Nicole met with rejection at the plastic surgeon's office, Maureen tried to cheer her up by taking her to Malibu
to go surfing.

While Nicole managed to get up on a surfboard only once for about fifteen seconds, she immediately decided that surfing was totally for her, especially after she visited one of the surf shops on the beach. The store carried a huge array of bathing suits, shorts, halter-tops, and sandals, and Nicole nearly maxed out her credit card with all of her purchases.

When she got back to Delta City, Nicole didn't talk much about her abortive attempt at a boob job, but she did talk almost constantly about surfing.

"Barbara, Cairn, you simply cannot imagine how it feels to be on your board riding a wave. It gives you such a sense of freedom and of being one with the ocean."

In her typically direct fashion, Barbara said, "Nicole, you were only in L.A. for four days. Exactly how much surfing did you do?"

"Well, I did a hell of a lot more surfing than you and Cairn did sitting on your butts here in Delta City."

Suddenly Cairn let out a scream and said, "Goddamn it, I give up."

Nicole and Barbara stared at her as she continued, "My name is Karen. K-A-R-E-N, KA-REN! Why is it that nobody in Delta City can say it right? All I hear is 'Cairn' this and 'Cairn' that, so I just give up. When we go back to school in the fall I'm going to just register as Cairn and be done with it!"

Since it had now been nearly fifteen seconds since she had been the center of attention, Nicole said, "You do whatever you want to when we go back to school, Cairn. But right now we're talking about surfing." Seeing a movement outside her bedroom door, she said, "Hi, Ray."

Nicole's older brother, Ray Dean, Jr., stuck his head in the door and began singing "Do you love me, do you, Surfer Girl?"

Merlene Bailey, the family matriarch, called out, "Is that you singing, Ray Dean? I always loved it when that little band you had in high school played those Beach Boys songs."

"Yeah, Mom. Cairn and Barbara are in here with Nicole, and I'm just giving a little performance for the Surfer Girls."

So that fall it was Nicole, Barbara, and Cairn, the Surfer Girls, who returned to Delta City High School.

CHAPTER 15

Like a lot of the men and women who wear a uniform, Dan Arthur Truman not only often spoke in the same jargon he used in his police reports, he actually thought in that same language.

So it wasn't his pickup truck that he pulled into the parking space behind the Delta City Police Department building, it was his "personal vehicle".

Dan Arthur was proud of the truck, the first brand new vehicle he had ever been able to buy. It was a light blue Ford and Dan Arthur kept it spotless inside and out.

A really great deal on the truck had come his way a couple of weeks after the man who owned the Ford dealership had a few too many while playing golf at the country club. Dan Arthur had given the car dealer a ride home instead of a DUI ticket and the dealer had shown his appreciation with a special discount on the truck.

Dan Arthur arrived at the police department shortly before ten o'clock, well before his three p.m. to eleven p.m. patrol shift, but Chief Laird had asked him to have a chat with Donnie Taylor.

Like most cops, Dan Arthur could act quickly when it was required, but whenever possible he liked to consider all of the facts and alternatives before taking action.

So, he had spent the weekend putting together a game plan for interrogating Donnie.

Dan Arthur decided that he would talk to Donnie on Monday morning. There wouldn't be many customers at Delta City Appliance World, so Donnie wouldn't have any problem getting away, and Dan Arthur figured that by talking to Donnie early in the day he might be able to catch him off guard.

Seeing Donnie's car parked behind Delta City Appliance World, Dan Arthur hurried in to the police station to clock in. Dan Arthur really didn't need to punch the time clock since he would not receive any overtime pay for the work he would be doing today, but the extra hours would look good on his record. Delta City never paid its employees for overtime work simply because there wasn't any money for it in the town's budget.

Despite its name, Delta City was just an ordinary small Southern town. While the 2000 census had shown a population of 5,202, the "Welcome to Delta City – Population" signs at the city limits now read 8,702.

The city fathers were sure that Delta City was always growing, so each year they arbitrarily added 500 to the population signs. And when the new census came out every ten years the population numbers would have to be drastically lowered, because from about 1950 on Delta City's population had always been somewhere between 4,700 and 5,300. But that didn't stop the city fathers, who just kept on adding 500 additional people to the sign every year.

There were a handful of wealthy families in Delta City, and a slightly larger number of poor people, although the poor people really weren't *that* poor. Delta City had an attitude that if someone didn't want to work, they should move somewhere else, but as long as a person worked, Delta City would make sure they managed to get by. And it was a point of pride that Delta City took care of its own without depending on money from the Federal government to do it, although the city fathers were more than happy to scoop up whatever funds might flow from Washington.

But most of the folks in Delta City were solid middle class. Husbands and wives both worked, and that allowed them to have a nice house, along with a new car every couple of years.

One thing just about everybody in Delta City agreed on was the role of local government. It should provide police and fire protection, pave the roads, and operate the schools. It should do these things as cheaply as possible, then it should stay out of people's lives. And they made sure that local government did stay out of their lives when they went to the voting booth. They could accept the occasional tax increase, after all everything always cost more than it did the year before, but if a city councilman wanted to raise taxes to pay for something outside the narrow mandate of the people he would quickly be an ex-city councilman.

Although the lean budget meant that city workers didn't get overtime pay, the people of Delta City contributed to a City Workers Appreciation Fund. The fund gave out bonuses every Christmas, and if the public servants had been called on to work a lot of extra hours that year their bonuses would be slightly more generous.

But Dan Arthur Truman didn't work for the Delta City Police Department to get rich. He worked there because the five thousand and however many people who lived there were his people. He'd known a great many of them most of their lives, and he believed that he could keep them safer than anyone else could.

After punching the time clock, Dan Arthur walked down a hall to a door marked "CSI". He smiled as he walked into the room, which was still pretty much just a place for junk that the police department didn't have anywhere else to store. However, a cleaned-up corner of the room now held a few modern investigative tools.

Federal money had paid for the video equipment, the chemicals to detect blood spatters, the evidence collection kits, and all of the other equipment. One thing Chief Laird was good at was taking advantage of whatever largess Uncle Sam might make available.

With the new equipment had come a need for someone who knew how to use it, and the City Council had grudgingly come up with the money for Dan Arthur to spend a week at FBI headquarters in Virginia.

While almost everybody in Delta City knew that Dan Arthur had only barely made it through high school, very few of them knew that he was now one of the best-trained police officers in the state of Arkansas.

Dan Arthur had never planned to be a police officer. In fact, he had never planned to be much of anything. For most of his life, one Bigfoot Newton had represented "the cops", and up until just before Dan Arthur's high school graduation, Bigfoot Newton had not represented anything Dan Arthur found interesting.

CHAPTER 16

Bigfoot Newton had come back from Vietnam in 1974 and gone to work for the Delta City Police Department. In less than five years, his lithe soldier's body had ballooned to nearly 350 pounds. He was so heavy that the patrol car he normally drove had a permanent lean toward the driver's side.

Bigfoot had good instincts. He knew who was good, who was going through a phase, and who was genuinely bad. Moreover, he knew that the night he caught the mayor parked on a dirt road with his pants down and one of the football players from Delta City University between his legs that his patrol log should show that he was clear on the other side of town at the time.

By 1983, the high school kids who were gathered one night on the parking lot of Mike's Restaurant looked on Bigfoot as just a fat annoyance. The Surfer Girls were there, with Donnie Taylor just a few feet away. Dan Arthur was there, as were most of the other young men and women who were anxiously awaiting their graduation from Delta City High School, less than a month away.

The kids weren't surprised to see Bigfoot pull his patrol car into the parking lot. He usually came through a couple of times a night just to let the kids know that he had his eye on them. However, they were surprised when he pulled up right next to them and started to get out of the car. Despite the large feet that had given him his nickname, everybody in town knew that he far preferred sitting to standing.

"Evenin', kids."

There was a brief buzz as everyone tried to remember the cop's last name, finally one of the kids muttered, "How ya doing, Officer Bigfoot?"

The policeman gave a tight smile, then continued, "Kids, I don't want to spoil your fun, but it might be a good idea if ya'll headed on home now."

There was a collective groan from the kids, then Bigfoot said, "It's not a problem with ya'll. There was four murderers that escaped from prison up by Pine Bluff, and the State Police say they're headed this way. It would just be better if you kids weren't around if they come through here."

One boy, filled with whiskey courage, muttered, "If them sum-bitches come up by me I'll kick their fuckin' asses!"

Bigfoot gave him a cold stare and asked, "I wouldn't find a bottle of liquor if I was to feel up under the front seat of your car, would I?"

The boy's bravado left like the air from a punctured balloon. He quickly looked around the crowd, and seeing a boy he knew didn't drink, he quickly asked, "Joe, could you drive me home in my car? My leg's bothering me just a little bit."

Bigfoot gave another tight smile, and returned to addressing the group of kids, "C'mon now, ya'll head on home. You can come back out tomorrow night. I just don't want any of you getting hurt or…" His voice trailed off as he heard an excited call from the police radio in his patrol car. Stepping back to the car, Bigfoot picked up the microphone, spoke briefly, then turned toward the kids and yelled, "Go home, now!" Jumping into his patrol car, he turned on the blue light and siren, and then sped out of the parking lot and turned onto El Dorado Road, which ran west out of Delta City.

The group of kids dutifully got in their cars and headed home. All except for Dan Arthur. After waiting for a couple of minutes he headed out in the direction taken by Bigfoot in his squad car.

There was a small hill just outside of town, and as he topped it, Dan Arthur saw an amazing sight.

Bigfoot's patrol car was blocking the highway, with the front bumper nearly torn off. Another car was upside down off the side of the road, where it had landed after striking the police car. At the edge of the highway, four men were laying face down on the gravel shoulder with their hands clasped behind their heads and at their feet was Bigfoot, covering them with a shotgun.

As Dan Arthur slowed his car at the scene, Bigfoot raised the shotgun toward him. Recognizing him, Bigfoot called out, "Dan Arthur, can you help me out for a minute?"

"Sure thing."

"Just go over to my patrol car and pick up the radio microphone. Press that button on the side and just start talking. Say where we're at, and then tell them to send the State Police."

Dan Arthur nodded and walked toward the police car. Picking up the microphone, he took a deep breath and said, "This here's Dan Arthur Truman. I'm out here on El Dorado Road about two miles west of Mike's place. Officer Bigfoot has some prisoners and wants me to have ya'll call the State Police."

A voice came back, "Sir, I have your message. Tell Officer Newton that the State Police are about five minutes away. Then you need to get well back in case Officer Newton has to use his weapon."

Dan Arthur put down the microphone and yelled, "The State Police will be here in about five minutes!"

Bigfoot yelled back, "Okay, stay there behind my car."

Just about the time Dan Arthur's heart rate returned to normal he heard sirens and saw blue lights coming from both directions.

One of the state policemen came over to Dan Arthur and asked, "You the fellow that called for backup for Officer Newton?"

"Yessir, I did it just like he told me to."

Patting him on the shoulder, the cop said, "Good job, son. Pull your car off the road while I help get these bad guys under control, then I'll need to take a statement from you."

Sitting on the hood of his car while waiting to give his statement, Dan Arthur was amazed when one of the state policemen began picking up guns from where Bigfoot had piled them and he saw that Bigfoot had taken six pistols off the four criminals.

One of the other policemen was examining Bigfoot's face with a flashlight and Dan Arthur heard him say, "Looks like you're gonna have quite a shiner there Newton. What happened?"

"Well, I had to jump back when they nicked my cruiser, then I went running up there when their car rolled over. Just as I got up there, one old boy who'd crawled out jumped up and hit me then took off running. He made it about twenty feet before I got my nightstick on him, but after that he settled on down. I walked him back here just as the other boys were crawling out of the car, so I just put my shotgun on them and told them to line up there on the shoulder of the road."

The state policeman laughed, then came over to Dan Arthur and said, "Now tell me about your part in all of this."

Dan Arthur briefly recounted the events, starting with Bigfoot's stopping by Mike's to warn the kids, and ending with his call on the police car's radio.

When Dan Arthur finished, the state policeman smiled and said, "Officially I have to tell you that it's a crime to follow a police car, but unofficially I'm glad you did. Thanks for your help. Now you better head on home before your parents get worried."

A couple of days later there was a special assembly at Delta City High School and when he entered the auditorium, Dan Arthur was surprised to see several policemen on the stage. He was even more surprised when the policemen called him up and gave him a special commendation for helping Bigfoot.

Dan Arthur endured a few days of "Officer Truman" and "Dudley Doright" taunts, but an idea was growing in his head.

Shortly after high school graduation, Dan Arthur reported for Army boot camp. He later attended the Military Police School at Ft. Leonard Wood, then spent the rest of his military career doing everything from guarding nuclear weapons to hauling drunk soldiers out of bars.

After his four years in the military, Dan Arthur returned to Delta City, joined the Police Department, and married the girl he had dated in high school. While the career took, the marriage didn't.

Unburdened by any family responsibilities, Dan Arthur threw himself into his job. If a book or article had information about professional police work, he read it. If a seminar or class on police work was available, he took it. If there was a law enforcement convention, he was there, even if he had to pay for it out of his own pocket.

His educational efforts turned him into a first-class law enforcement officer, but the things Dan Arthur learned from Bigfoot Newton in his early days as a policeman were what made him a good small town cop.

CHAPTER 17

In the CSI room, Dan Arthur sat down in front of some videotape equipment. Mike's Restaurant and the University Club had installed security cameras aimed at their entrances and parking lots. However, one camera at the University Club had been knocked around so many times that it now pointed straight up at the sky. Looking at the tape from that camera, Dan Arthur laughingly thought, *"If we're ever attacked by enemy bombers we'll have a damn good view of them."*

Picking up a legal pad, Dan Arthur wrote a quick note to Chief Laird suggesting that the chief try to convince the owners of Mike's Restaurant and the University Club to have the cameras re-aimed.

Dan Arthur had thoroughly reviewed the videotapes Friday evening after his patrol shift, but he wanted to give them one last look before he talked to Donnie. While he hoped he might find something on the tapes that he had missed before, more realistically he was looking for anything he might be able to use to get Donnie to open up about what, if anything, he might know.

His review of the videotapes finished, Dan Arthur came out into the hall and noticed that the CSI nameplate on the door had picked up a very obvious fingerprint. When the police department first received the new investigative equipment, a Storage Room sign was on the door. However, when Dan Arthur came back from his FBI training he found the CSI sign installed, and assumed one of the other police officers had put it up in honor of the TV shows of the same name.

At least once a week Dan Arthur would find some sort of faux evidence on the CSI sign. Sometimes it was a large fingerprint, other times it was some clothing fibers or a few hairs, and on a couple of occasions he found what appeared to be some sort of bodily fluids whose source he didn't particularly care to speculate about.

Donnie Taylors's mother, who co-owned the store, greeted Dan Arthur when he walked through the front door of Delta City Appliance World.

"Dan Arthur, you know Monday is always a sale day. I can give you a really good deal on that big-screen TV you've been looking at!"

"Mrs. Taylor, I know you always give me a bargain, but I'm afraid that if the price is much over fifty cents it would break my budget today. Actually, I just came by to talk to Donnie."

Saying, "He's back in the stockroom," Mrs. Taylor picked up a nearby phone and paged him.

A minute or so later Donnie emerged from the rear of the store heartily exclaiming, "Officer Truman! I hope Mom told you we could give you a great price on a big screen today."

"Donnie, your mother's probably the best salesperson in town, but I'm afraid I can't quite swing it right now. Actually, I was hoping we could walk over to Tommy's Diner and have a cup of coffee."

Donnie's mother interjected, "You mean Café on the Square. You know Tommy's son changed the name after his Daddy died."

Dan Arthur laughed and said, "Well, it was Tommy's Diner when I was born, and as far as I'm concerned it will always be Tommy's diner. So how about it, Mrs. Taylor, are you going to let Donnie slip off for a few minutes?"

"For you, Dan Arthur, anything. Donnie, you run along with Dan Arthur and I'll mind the store until you get back."

Donnie knew that he wasn't breaking any laws with his constant shadowing of the Surfer Girls, but he was always a little reticent around law enforcement officers.

As the two men turned to leave, Dan Arthur thought he saw the slightest twinge of concern on Donnie's face.

CHAPTER 18

Donnie was somewhat puzzled by Dan Arthur's coffee invitation even though he got along well with all of Delta City's policemen who all seemed quite willing to overlook his obsession with the Surfer Girls as long as he stayed inside the boundaries of the law and the girls didn't complain. But despite the good relationship, Donnie had never really socialized with any of the town's police officers.

Donnie had never really understood why he was so fixated on Nicole, Barbara, and Cairn. True, they had been among the prettiest and most popular girls in school, and all of the boys had lusted after them in some fashion or another.

But what Donnie felt for the Surfer Girls was nothing so cheap as either lust or love. It was pure adoration, much as someone would have for a movie star or a spiritual figure.

Donnie had watched from the sidelines over the years as the Surfer Girls, oblivious to his presence, dated and slept with other boys, but he always tried to stand or sit close to them, hoping that simple proximity might someday cause at least one of the Surfer Girls to notice him.

Once, when he and the Surfer Girls were still in high school, it had almost happened.

Barbara was carrying a large stack of books when one of them slipped. When she tried to grab it, all of the other books went flying.

Hurriedly gathering the books, Donnie handed them to Barbara with a big smile. Unfortunately, Barbara seemed to be lost in another world. Taking the books from Donnie, she said, "Thanks, David," and walked away.

Other young men would have simply said a mental "fuck you" and walked away, while vowing either to forget about the Surfer Girls or to start plotting some childish act of revenge.

Donnie, however, was made of sterner stuff. He just kept smiling and thought, *"At least she knew my name started with a 'D'."*

Then, shortly after his high school graduation, Donnie lost his virginity with the first and only real girlfriend he ever had.

Sue Carol Raines, now the waitress at Café on the Square, was 15 at the time and given to loudly proclaiming, "There's only two things to do in Delta City, drink and fuck, and I don't like booze!"

And she engaged in the latter activity as often as possible.

As was often the case on summer evenings, most of the students at Delta City High School had gathered on the parking lot at Mike's Restaurant, and since the Surfer Girls were there, Donnie was also there.

When the group began to disperse at the end of the evening, Sue Carol asked Donnie for a ride home. The Surfer Girls were going off with their boyfriends de jour, so Donnie reluctantly said okay.

Sue Carol lived way out in the country, and about halfway to her house she said, "Donnie, pull over for a minute."

"Why?"

"Cause I have to pee."

Donnie pulled to the side of the road, and Sue Carol jumped out and walked behind some bushes.

When she returned, Donnie started to put the car in drive, but Sue Carol grabbed the gearshift. Donnie turned to look at her and noticed that her jeans and shoes were on the floor of the car, and that she was naked from the waist down.

Donnie was almost in shock as Sue Carol opened his belt, unzipped his jeans, and yanked them down. Pulling out his penis, Sue Carol bent down and began giving Donnie a blowjob.

Thirty seconds later Donnie's penis was not responding, so Sue Carol said in a taunting voice, "I'll bet if it was Nicole or Barbara or Cairn sucking your dick it'd be sticking straight up by now!"

The effect of her words was amazing. As Sue Carol spat out each of the Surfer Girl's names, Donnie's penis got incrementally harder, and by the time she finished her sentence it was standing up straight and tall.

Surveying his erection for a moment, Sue Carol said, "Now that's much better," and climbed on top of him.

Donnie felt torn by what was happening to him, as he had always believed that he was saving himself for the Surfer Girls. In his heart, Donnie felt that he was betraying the Surfer Girls, but in his cock, the feeling was incredible.

The thought of betrayal made his penis soften slightly, and Sue Carol said, "Goddammit, Donnie! Don't you quit on me now! Just pretend you're fucking Cairn. That'll get you hard again!"

Her words had the desired effect, so Sue Carol kept the fantasy going. "Doesn't it feel good having your dick sliding in and out of Barbara's pussy? Isn't it great having Nicole's cunt wrapped around your cock?"

A few seconds later Donnie's penis erupted inside a moaning and screaming Sue Carol.

Since then, both the sex and Sue Carol's "Surfer Girls" routine had been repeated on an almost weekly basis, with only a brief interruption for Sue Carol's short-lived marriage. Sue Carol would pretend to be one or more of the Surfer Girls, sometimes even dressing like one of them, and a hyper-stimulated Donnie would sometimes fuck her for hours.

Of course, Donnie never knew that Sue Carol told all of the girls in her gym class the gory details about their sex life, and that just about everybody in town now knew all about it.

Including Dan Arthur.

CHAPTER 19

Dan Arthur smiled inwardly as he and Donnie walked into Café on the Square, as it was no accident that they would be having coffee at this particular time of day and in this location.

Leading the way to a table by the front window, Dan Arthur smiled as the waitress came over to take their order and said, "How ya doin', Sue Carol?"

"Just fine, Dan Arthur. Hi, Donnie. You guys just want coffee?"

Dan Arthur replied, "I don't know about Donnie, but I'm going to exercise my cop's prerogative and also have a donut."

"No problem. Donnie, we've got some of those brownies that you like so much. You want me to bring you one?"

Donnie brusquely replied, "No, just the coffee."

"*Good, good,*" thought Dan Arthur as he watched the exchange. He had deliberately chosen to sit in the section of the café where Sue Carol worked, hoping her presence might knock Donnie a little off guard. Even though everybody in town knew about the relationship between Donnie and Sue Carol, he always tried to give the impression that they were barely acquaintances.

There was actually no need for Dan Arthur to play all of these cop games, as he really didn't believe that Donnie would be able to provide any useful information about the car thief. However, because of all of his police training, he knew that he could gain an advantage by keeping anyone he questioned just a little bit uncomfortable. Then there's always the old "good cop – bad cop" game.

"So, when are ya'll going to be getting in some 60 inch plasma TVs, Donnie?"

"Well, Dan Arthur, folks are kinda holding on to their money right now, so I'm gonna wait for the prices to drop a bit more before I stock any, but I can always special order one for you, Dan Arthur."

The cop replied, "No sense tying up money in inventory you can't sell I guess." Laughing, he continued, "Course that means if I get a wild hair up my ass and decide I want one right now I'll have to head up to Pine Bluff to buy it."

"No need for that, Dan Arthur. You order it today and I can have UPS bring it to your door tomorrow. You remember I did that when the police department wanted that new video camera."

"Here ya go, boys," Sue Carol said as she placed two cups of coffee and a donut on the table. "Now don't start on that donut before I get my camera, Dan Arthur. I'll bet I could sell a picture of a cop eating a donut for a million dollars to one of them New York magazines!"

Dan Arthur reached for his handcuffs and said, "You just keep it up, Sue Carol and I'll put these on you in a heartbeat!"

"Oooh, Dan Arthur, if you're gonna start getting all sexy I'm going to leave." With a suggestive twitch of her hips, Sue Carol walked away.

Dan Arthur was looking at Sue Carol's retreating rear, but he was also stealthily observing Donnie out of the corner of his eyes and said, "Ya know Donnie, I've never understood why Sue Carol never got married again after what's-his-name ran out on her. A woman that pretty and sweet shouldn't have to be alone all the time." He observed a barely visible tightening of Donnie's jaw and thought, *"Gotcha!"*

Now, good cop. "I'm hoping you might be able to help me out, Donnie. You heard about that fella that left the stolen Mercedes in the University Club's parking lot Monday night?"

Donnie replied, "Yeah, I saw the article in the paper yesterday."

Dan Arthur continued, "I kinda remember seeing you driving around town that night, and I wondered if you might have seen anything suspicious."

"Sorry, Dan Arthur. I don't recall seeing anything out of the ordinary."

"Well Donnie, you know they've got video cameras at Mike's Restaurant and at the University Club. I was looking at the tapes and I saw a couple of interesting things."

Donnie's face briefly clouded, but he quickly forced a laugh and said, "Unless the thief parachuted into the University Club parking lot I don't think the cameras could see very much. I keep telling them they need to adjust the cameras but they're too damn cheap to do it. Did you see anything that will help you find the guy?"

"That depends on how much help you can give me. When I was looking at the tape from Mike's I could see you sitting out at the edge of the restaurant's parking lot, and from the time stamps on the tapes that was around the time the car thief was pulling into the University Club parking lot."

Donnie just took a sip of coffee and nodded his head, but Dan Arthur noticed that the hand holding the cup was trembling slightly.

Dan Arthur continued, "I didn't get much from the tapes at the University Club. I can kinda see the stolen Mercedes pulling into the parking lot, and a few seconds later Cairn Dumont's car pulls out of the lot."

Taking another sip of coffee, Donnie said, "I didn't notice anything out of the ordinary. But I really wasn't paying that much attention."

Dan Arthur decided to go with one more good jolt of bad cop, but he wrapped it in a smile as he said, "Bullshit, Donnie! If there's a Surfer Girl within ten miles you're watching every move they make. So I know you were watching when Cairn left the University Club. She didn't by any chance have somebody with her when she left, did she?"

Donnie's face went cold as some pieces began to fall into place. He had seen Cairn pick up a strange man in the parking lot of the University Club, and he had read about the car thief in the Delta City Journal, but he had not really drawn any connection between the two events. Even in Delta City there were bigger stories than a mere car thief. And he sure as hell didn't dwell on one of the Surfer Girls having fucked someone other than himself. One event dimmed, one event blocked, but now both brought forth in glaring juxtaposition.

Donnie suddenly realized that Dan Arthur wanted to know what he had seen because he suspected that Cairn might have been involved in the disappearance of the car thief.

Quickly forcing a smile, Donnie tried to focus on what the cop was saying.

"Sorry if I was a little rough on you there Donnie. With all of those TVs you've got around, I know you've seen how we play 'good cop - bad cop'. Sometimes it can shake loose something a person doesn't remember remembering."

Laughing, Donnie repeated, "Something a person doesn't remember remembering. Dan Arthur, I can almost hear that coming out of Andy Griffith's mouth. If all you're watching is 'Nick at Night' I can see where you don't want to invest in a good TV!"

Pleased that Donnie seemed to be recovering his good nature, Dan Arthur began sliding out of the booth and said, "Help me catch this bad guy, Donnie, and maybe I can get the city to give me a raise big enough to buy me a new TV."

Donnie also stood, saying, "If I don't get back to the store neither one of us will have money to buy much of anything!"

The cop replied, "I'll pay for the coffee. I can put it on my generous city expense account."

Donnie laughed and said, "Well pay up and let's get out of here!"

Dan Arthur nodded toward the waitress and said, "Go ahead on, Donnie. I've got a few things I need to ask Sue Carol about."

Donnie's face was tight as he walked toward Delta City Appliance World, but his mind was racing. He thought, *"You go ahead and talk to Sue Carol all you want to, Dan Arthur, and talk to anybody else you want to also. I don't know if Cairn was involved in this or not, but you can take me over to the police station and put me in the back room and pull my toenails out or whatever cops do and I still won't say anything that would hurt any of the Surfer Girls!"*

CHAPTER 20

Dan Arthur smiled at Donnie's abrupt departure from Café on the Square. He knew he was a good interrogator and he knew he had rattled Donnie. He wondered what sort of paranoia might be running through Donnie's brain because of his questioning.

Despite what the policeman had told Donnie, his "few things I need to ask Sue Carol about" were nothing more than ordinary old "How ya been doing" questions.

Dan Arthur hadn't really expected to get any useful information out of Donnie. As he had told Donnie, shaking loose something Donnie "didn't remember remembering" was the best he had hoped for.

And despite what Donnie might have thought, Dan Arthur really didn't think any of the Surfer Girls had been involved in the mysterious disappearance of the car thief.

CHAPTER 21

At Barbara's suggestion, the Surfer Girls had spent the weekend in Shreveport. As she had told Cairn, "It would do you good to just get out of town for a couple of days. And if Nicole gets drunk and starts running her mouth, nobody in Shreveport would have the slightest idea what she's talking about."

Now it was Monday, and the Surfer Girls were drinking margaritas on Nicole's patio.

From out of nowhere, Nicole asked, "Ya'll remember that year when we became witches?"

Barbara almost choked on her drink as she asked, "How many margaritas have we had? Where the hell did that come from?"

CHAPTER 22

The year the Surfer Girls had become witches was 1980, when they were all 15-year old tenth graders. It was late September, and the girls were sitting in the front yard of Nicole's house watching Nicole's father and brother installing the very elaborate Halloween decorations that were a seasonal trademark of the Bailey home.

As the two men were putting a large figure of a witch on the roof, Cairn idly said, "That's not the way witches really looked."

Nicole snapped, "And just what makes you think you know what witches really looked like, Cairn?"

Barbara interjected, "If you'd quit reading all of those wedding magazines and pick up a history book you'd know about the Salem Witch Trials and all of that."

Nicole replied, "I know all about that. It was in North Carolina where they make Salem cigarettes."

The other two girls erupted in laughter. After a few seconds Barbara recovered enough to say, "No, dumbass. The Salem Witch Trials were in Massachusetts. You know, like where Cairn is from?"

Cairn jumped in, "And Salem was only about an hour away from where I lived. We used to go over there a lot around Halloween. They've got stores where they sell witch shit, and witch museums. Witches looked just like all of the rest of the Pilgrim women, or whatever they were. They didn't wear those stupid hats, and the only time they had a broomstick was when they were sweeping. I've got some books from Salem I'll show you next time we're over at my house."

Nicole jumped up and said, "Let's go over there and look at those books right now."

The other two girls exchanged smiles, knowing that Nicole's suggestion was driven less by intellectual curiosity and more by what was sitting in the driveway.

Over the summer, Nicole's mother had gotten tired of chauffeuring her daughter around and had convinced her husband to buy Nicole a car. Even though Nicole was still a year short of the sixteen years she needed to obtain her driver's license, Mrs. Bailey reasoned that fifteen was close enough. And since the Delta City police knew that her husband's money gave him the ability to affect their jobs, they wisely decided to accept Mrs. Bailey's reasoning.

The Surfer Girls jumped into Nicole's bright red Mustang convertible and headed for the world of the occult that awaited them at Cairn's house.

CHAPTER 23

Taking a sip of her margarita, Cairn asked, "Nicole, what on earth prompted you to think about that witch stuff?"

Nicole replied, "I don't know. With the dead guy and all I've just been thinking about something."

"Oh, shit!" the other two women muttered in unison. They both held the opinion that Nicole and thinking was a dangerous combination.

"No, seriously, ya'll," Nicole responded. "Think about it. We killed that guy that's in Cairn's freezer 'cause he tried to make Cairn suck his dick."

Barbara responded, "No, Nicole, it wasn't any 'we' that killed him, and Cairn didn't kill him on purpose, it was totally an accident."

In a low voice Nicole asked, "Well, what about Bobby Ellis?"

Barbara almost screamed, "Goddamn it, Nicole! We swore none of us would ever mention his name again!"

And there had never really been any reason to mention Bobby's name since that day in November 1980 when he died.

By that time, the Surfer Girl's coven was in full swing. They'd started with the books Cairn had brought with her from Massachusetts, then called one of the stores in Salem and bought more books, along with some witch accessories, much of which consisted of various parts of dead animals.

They lit their candles and did their chants, and enough coincidences came along to convince the Surfer Girls that they had tapped into some sort of supernatural power. While they truly believed a power failure was the result of their incantations, the linemen from Arkansas Power

& Light knew that it was squirrels chewing on the electric lines that had made the lights go out.

The Surfer Girls had an unspoken pact to keep their coven a secret at school, but one day Nicole accidentally dropped her stack of books, and the boy who helped her pick them up noticed she was carrying a book about witchcraft. The story quickly made the rounds of Delta City High School, but due to their parent's money and power, the Surfer Girls enjoyed a certain untouchable status, and the discussion of their occult hobby fizzled out almost as soon as it began.

CHAPTER 24

The Friday afternoon before the high school football team's state championship game, the school administration gave up on teaching anything and allowed a spontaneous pep rally to get underway.

Bobby Ellis was the quarterback of the Delta City Gators, which gave him a certain amount of status among the 400 other students there, and that status gave him a certain amount of attitude.

With the football team lined up behind him on the front steps of the school, Bobby began giving the obligatory speech.

"I want all of you to know that me and the rest of the guys on the team are super-pumped, and we're going to go out on the field tonight and kick ass!" Bobby smiled briefly at the disapproving look he got from the principal over his use of the word "ass", then continued, "and then we're going to the state championships and kick ass there, too!"

The crowd in front of the school began chanting, "Go Gators go Gators."

Bobby let the chanting continue for a minute or so, then raised his hands for silence and said, "It takes a great team to win, but we can't do it by ourselves. We've got to have great support from everybody at school, and you guys give us the greatest."

Again, the chanting of "Go Gators!" erupted, but Bobby cut it short with another wave of his hands.

Glancing around the crowd, Bobby saw the Surfer Girls, and said, "Let me show you a great example of school spirit." He pointing to Barbara, and said "Come on up here for a minute."

After a quick glance at Nicole and Cairn, Barbara walked up the steps. Bobby guided her to the step in front of him, and stood behind her with his hands on her shoulders.

"You guys all know Barbara. She's one of the Surfer Girls."

There was a brief chant of "Surfer Girls, Surfer Girls," which Bobby quickly cut off, saying, "And Barbara is one of those people who truly know what school spirit is all about. She's in the stands cheering at all of the games, she makes the banners for the pep rallies, and she's always ready to do whatever she can to help the Gators!"

Bobby continued, "And I know Barbara is going to do everything she can today to help us win tonight's game. I just found out that she and the other Surfer Girls have taken up witchcraft, so I'm sure she won't mind giving me a double handful of witch's tit for good luck!" With that, he dropped his hands from Barbara's shoulders and grabbed her breasts.

Barbara was mortified, and stood stock still for a moment. Even during her hottest and heaviest makeout sessions, she hadn't yet allowed anybody to feel her up. Now, it had just happened in front of the whole school.

She reacted instinctively, turning and swinging a closed fist toward Bobby's face. He jerked back, but Barbara's hand managed to deliver a grazing blow to his left eye.

One of the other players grabbed Bobby, Cairn came up and pulled Barbara away, and the principal began breaking up the crowd.

Jody Raymond, the school guidance counselor, came over to Barbara and said, "I'll have Bobby in my office first thing Monday morning, and I will give him the severest punishment I possibly can. Nicole, why don't you and Cairn take Barbara home and just relax for a while. But, believe me, Bobby will pay for this Monday!"

CHAPTER 25

Thirty minutes later, Barbara was standing in her bathroom carefully examining her breasts. She found a couple of tiny-little-might-be-the-beginnings-of-a-bruises, but nothing that constituted a serious injury. Putting her bra and shirt back on she returned to her bedroom where Nicole and Cairn were waiting.

"Your boobs okay?" Nicole asked.

Cairn cattily said, "Unlike some people here, I think Barbara is probably worried about a little more than just her tits."

Barbara said, "They're okay, but Cairn's right. Everybody at school is going to think I'm some kind of slut for letting him feel me up, even though I didn't want him to."

Cairn said, "Just try not to think about it. You know how Ms. Raymond feels about shit like that, and I don't think she likes Bobby much in the first place. She'll nail his ass to the wall."

"Don't bank on it," Nicole interjected. "Bobby Ellis may be a total piece of shit, but he can play football. He'll win the game tonight, and by Monday, everybody will be talking about how Bobby led the school to the state championships. About all Ms. Raymond will be able to do is bitch at him some."

Barbara responded, "Well that's not enough for me. I'm gonna fuck him up good and ya'll are going to help me."

Five minutes later the lights were off, the candles lit, and the Surfer Girls coven was in full-blown getting even mode. They hadn't been able to find a specific incantation that would cause someone to lose a football game, so they just picked the closest one they could find and began chanting.

CHAPTER 26

It wasn't the Surfer Girl's incantation that made Bobby miss the critical pass that cost the Gator's the game. Just before he threw the ball, the eye where Barbara had hit him went fuzzy for a second. His pass was off the mark, and the Gators went home winless.

Around one o'clock the next afternoon the Surfer Girls were standing in front of Nicole's Mustang, on the parking lot at Mike's Restaurant.

Normally the lot would be full on the afternoon following a big game, but today it was almost deserted. Besides the Surfer Girls, the only other person there was Donnie Taylor, who was just coming out of Mike's with some food, and as usual, they never even saw him. They'd just finished eating lunch and were half-heartedly passing around a joint.

"Why do we smoke pot anyway?" Nicole asked. "It don't do a thing for me."

Cairn wryly responded, "Me either. You guys want to get another large order of fries?"

Barbara, who had just taken in a lungful of smoke, started laughing and coughing at the same time, and then said, "Stop it, you're gonna make me die!" Looking up and seeing a yellow Honda sedan pull into the parking lot, Barbara said, "Motherfucker!"

Bobby Ellis pulled his Honda right up to where the Surfer Girls were standing, rolled down his window, and started screaming, "You stupid cunts! Bitch Barbara made me lose the game! Now my Daddy's going to have to pay for me to go to college instead of me going on a football scholarship, and he's totally pissed."

Ignoring his rant, Barbara turned to Nicole and Cairn and said, "Start chanting. And this time it's not about a stupid football game, I want Bobby Ellis to die!"

"Cunts!" Bobby yelled and started driving toward the parking lot exit.

Just as he reached the edge of the highway, Nicole suddenly yanked up her shirt and bra and screamed, "You want some witch's tits, motherfucker? Here's some for you!"

Bobby pulled out onto the highway, was t-boned by a large tractor-trailer, and died instantly.

CHAPTER 27

As Barbara took a sip of her margarita she thought, *"My God, it's been nearly twenty-five years since Bobby Ellis died."*

Cairn was saying, "Nicole, you're nuts. That witchcraft shit we did in high school was just a silly game. Nothing ever happened because of those spells we cast."

Nicole responded, "Well, we did an incantation and it made Bobby Ellis throw a bad pass and lose the football game."

Barbara said, "No, Nicole. Bobby screwed up his pass because he was having trouble seeing. Remember, I hit him in the eye after he grabbed my tits. If you'd actually been watching the game you would have seen him shaking his head like he was trying to clear it before he threw the ball."

Nicole continued, "Well, we were chanting when Bobby pulled out in front of that 18-wheeler and got hit."

Cairn jumped in, "Correction! Barbara and I were chanting, you were flashing your tits at him. That probably scared him so bad that he hit the gas instead of the brake."

Nicole mused, "I bet that was the first time that little shit had ever actually seen a woman's boobs, so I suppose I might have distracted him a little bit when I flashed him."

Barbara almost screamed, "Oh bullshit, Nicole! You know that the only girls who got on the cheerleader squad were girls who fucked Bobby, or at least gave him a blowjob. I imagine he'd seen a tit or two before you flashed him. It was probably just seeing your boobs that scared him. You remember how you hauled them out in front of everybody at the country club's New Year's Eve dance last year, and how the mayor said you had the scariest tits he'd ever seen?"

Cairn began to laugh as Nicole spluttered, "There is nothing wrong with my boobs! They're a lot better than either of you have!"

Cairn suddenly turned serious, saying, "Do you suppose anyone ever found out about Nicole flashing Bobby right before he pulled out in front of that truck?"

Barbara replied, "I don't think so. When the cops questioned everybody at Mike's nobody said anything about it, so I guess nobody saw it."

Nicole chimed in, "And there was nobody but us outside," completely unaware that Donnie had been less than twenty feet from her.

Barbara said, "Well, I always hoped that Bobby didn't see Nicole. I was major pissed off about him grabbing my boobs, but I didn't really want to kill him or anything."

Nicole shook her chest and said, "If I had 'em out, you can bet he saw them!"

In fact, Bobby had not seen Nicole. He had been carefully looking both ways before pulling out onto the highway, had seen the truck, and had his foot firmly on the brake pedal. And he could only scream "Nooooo!" as his car started moving inexorably into the path of the truck.

Although the Surfer Girls had been oblivious to his presence, Donnie had been there the day Bobby Ellis died, and he had seen Nicole flash him.

When the cops got to Mike's Restaurant, Donnie had carefully maneuvered so that he could hear what everybody else was telling them about the accident, and he made sure that he talked to the cops last. Nobody else had mentioned Nicole flashing Bobby, and he certainly wasn't going to. Nothing could ever make him betray the Surfer Girls.

Donnie had seen Nicole flash Bobby and had been transfixed. It was the first time he had actually seen a girl's breasts, and the fact that they belonged to one of the Surfer Girls was almost too good to be true. For Donnie, seeing one of the Surfer Girl's boobs for even a second was better than winning the lottery.

The minute he finished talking to the police Donnie almost ran to the restroom in Mike's Restaurant. Luckily, no one else felt the call of nature as he spent the next half hour furiously masturbating.

CHAPTER 28

Thursday night the Surfer Girls made their usual appearance at the University Club, where they would drink Jack Daniels and Coke all night long in preparation for the weekend.

Barbara had worried about Nicole getting drunk and running her mouth, and had discussed it with Cairn earlier in the day.

"I'm just not sure what to do about Nicole, Cairn."

Cairn wryly responded, "We could put her in the freezer with the dead guy. Then she could talk all she wanted to and nobody would be able to hear her."

Barbara laughed as she replied, "That's the problem, Cairn. If we don't go out like normal, people will start to talk. And if Nicole gets drunk there's no telling what she might say."

Cairn thought for a moment, then said, "I guess you and I are going to have to take turns staying sober and being something like a designated driver. Is there such a thing as a designated jailer?"

Barbara laughed again and said, "Designated jailer, I like that! But how are we going to explain one of us not drinking?"

Cairn replied, "I can handle things the rest of the week. I'll just tell everybody I'm taking antibiotics, and they won't work if I drink."

Barbara gave Cairn a hug and said, "Perfect. And I'll figure out something for next week."

Cairn returned the hug and wryly said, "For better or for worse, Surfer Girls forever!"

CHAPTER 29

At 11:45 p.m. the Surfer Girls were on their last drinks of the evening at the University Club when Nicole said, "I want to talk some more about that witchcraft stuff."

The other two women groaned in unison, and Barbara said, "Here we go again! Nicole, why in hell do you keep bringing that up?"

"Because I saw Randy Davis here in Delta City a couple of weeks ago! If he hadn't raped me and told everybody I was a slut back in high school I might have been able to marry at least one decent guy and have a nice life."

Barbara couldn't help but smile at the "at least one decent guy" comment. Nicole had been married and divorced three times before her twenty-third birthday, and none of her husbands had been stellar examples of humanity.

Unfortunately, about the only thing Nicole was qualified to do was be somebody's wife.

After losing a lot of money to husband number three, Nicole's father decided it would be cheaper to just give Nicole an allowance large enough for her to live well without a husband, and to open his checkbook for whatever charitable enterprises she could find to occupy her time.

As far as the rape went, both Barbara and Cairn had always considered it very much an "eye of the beholder" kind of thing.

CHAPTER 30

As the Surfer Girls finished their sophomore year in high school, their hormones were on the march and sex was a frequent topic of conversation.

One day they were hanging out at Barbara's house after school when Nicole said, "I've really been thinking about sex a lot lately."

Cairn responded, "Like the rest of us haven't been?"

Shooting her a nasty look, Nicole continued, "I mean, it sounds like it would be fun and all, but we really have to consider our positions."

Barbara interjected, "Doggie style sounds good to me!"

In an exasperated tone Nicole said, "Barbara, can you be serious for just one second? We're the Surfer Girls, and a lot of the other kids in town look up to us."

Barbara grinned at Cairn and said, "Oooh! That could be fun. Being on top with the guy looking up at you. He could suck your boobs while you were doing it!"

Nicole angrily replied, "Barbara, you may not have any self-respect, but some of us do."

Barbara said, "Okay, I'm sorry Nicole. What was it you wanted to say?"

Nicole replied, "Well, I just don't think the Surfer Girls should be the sluts of Delta City, and I think we should make a pact that none of us will have sex until we get out of high school."

Barbara and Cairn could barely avoid rolling their eyes as they glanced at each other, but Barbara managed to say, "Okay, if we all agree to save ourselves, I'll go along with it."

Cairn said, "I'm cool with that."

Nicole said, "I'm glad we got that decided. After all, we are the Surfer Girls and we need to set a good example for the other kids." Standing up, she continued, "I've got to go do some stuff for my mom, so I'll see you guys tomorrow."

Just as soon as Nicole's car pulled out of the driveway Cairn put on her best Nicole voice and said, "I think we should set a good example for the other kids!" Pulling up her shirt, she continued, "And here's a good example of what boobs look like!" Lowering her shirt she said, "Barbara, can you believe that shit?"

Barbara managed to contain her laughter long enough to say, "Cairn, you have got Nicole down perfectly!"

Cairn stood up and gave an exaggerated bow.

Barbara said, "I've only seen her flash a guy once. Has she done it more than that?"

"I don't think so. At least not yet. But it's just a matter of time with the way she drinks."

Barbara mused, "She'll flash her tits, but I bet she doesn't even jerk off. She'll probably be a cock teaser the rest of her life."

As Cairn nodded her head in agreement, Barbara asked, "Do you jerk off, Cairn?"

"Probably almost as much as you do, Barbara."

Both girls laughed, and Barbara said, "You know what this is really all about, don't you?"

Cairn asked, "What what is all about?"

"This whole virginity pact thing."

Cairn said, "I'm not sure. That whole setting a good example thing sounded a little fishy to me."

Barbara said, "What it's really about is Nicole doesn't want me or you to start fucking before she does. You know how she thinks she always has to be first to do stuff."

Cairn replied, "I hadn't thought of that. I should have known there was no way she would ever just act responsibly." Raising her voice she yelled, "Nicole, you're a self-centered bitch!"

When the two girls managed to stop laughing Barbara asked, "Are you going to stick with the virginity pledge, Cairn?"

"Hell no! I mean I'm not in any rush to get laid, but when I want to, I will, and I really don't give a shit what Nicole thinks about it. What about you?"

Barbara had pondered that question quite regularly when she was masturbating. Those little sessions with her pillow or her fingers felt very good, and she was really looking forward to the real thing.

Giving Cairn a serious look Barbara said, "I kinda feel the same way you do. I really want to find out what it's all about, but I don't want to just fuck the first guy that comes along." She paused for a moment, then grinned and said, "Maybe the second and the third and everybody else, but not the first guy that comes along. He'll have to just come alone!"

When Cairn stopped laughing she asked, "Barbara, where did you find out about that doggy style stuff and the woman being on top? I thought the guy was always on top."

Barbara said, "You remember a couple of months ago when Nicole was babysitting her brother's kids and I went over there to hang out? We were looking at his videotapes for something to watch and found a porno tape. I made a copy of it. Do you want to watch it?"

Cairn responded, "Hell yes! But I think you and I need to make a pact first."

Barbara looked at her quizzically and asked, "What kind of pact?"

Cairn grinned and said, "If you or I lose our virginity we'll tell each other, but we won't tell Nicole. Deal?"

Pulling the porn video out from under her bed, Barbara said, "Deal. Now let's get you educated!"

CHAPTER 31

While Nicole believed the Surfer Girls were bound by their virginity pact, the other girls at Delta City High School weren't, and many of them were quite sexually active.

Nicole, in an attempt to preserve her image of being the first to do everything, adopted the persona of a woman who had been having sex "like forever". She constantly commented on how the boys at school filled their jeans and made bawdy comments about what she'd like to do to them.

A week before the end of their sophomore year, the Surfer Girls had just finished their post-gym class showers when Cairn saw a ninth-grade girl edging toward Nicole.

Older students generally did not even acknowledge the existence of ninth-graders, and Nicole would certainly never notice one.

Defying her nonexistent status, the girl came right up to them and said, "Nicole?"

As usual, Nicole was making a point of talking to just about everyone in earshot while waiting far too long to put her bra on. Among themselves, Cairn and Barbara referred to these topless interludes as Nicole's "flasher practice".

A little louder, the girl said, "Nicole? You know Randy Davis?"

Nicole looked at the ninth-grader as if she had just dropped in from another planet, but she continued, "Randy's a friend of my brother, and I heard him saying the other day that he really hoped he could get together with you at Tina Nichol's end of school party."

Aware that all other conversation in the locker room had stopped, Nicole loudly replied, "Randy Davis? I saw him at the swimming pool and he's hung like a horse. If you see him again tell him that I'll be looking for him at Tina's and that I'm going to give him the ride of his life!"

The younger girl turned bright red, nodded her head, and hurried off.

As the Surfer Girls walked to their next class, Cairn said, "Nicole, if you keep talking shit like that one of these days somebody's going to take you up on it."

Nicole just smiled and said, "Oh shut up, Cairn! You and Barbara are just jealous because I'm going to get laid before ya'll do."

Behind Nicole's back, Barbara rolled her eyes at Cairn as they entered the classroom.

CHAPTER 32

Tina Nichol's parents had gone to Dallas for the weekend after telling Tina that she was not to have any parties, and if some of her friends dropped by there would be no pot smoking in the house.

Of course, before leaving, Tina's father had restocked the liquor cabinet and showed her how to operate the vent fan in the family's recreational vehicle.

The house was already full of well-on-their-way-to-being-drunk kids, when the Surfer Girls made their fashionably late appearance at nine p.m., while the dopers were making good use of the vent fan in the RV.

When the Surfer Girls entered, Tina came over and gave them an obligatory hug, then said, "Nicole, you bitch! I'll bet you went to Dallas for those white jeans, didn't you? I told mom to bring me back a couple of pairs this weekend."

Nicole replied, "Tina, this is the event of the year! You didn't think I'd show up for your party in something from the Gap or someplace, did you?"

Hearing Nicole's cloying words, Barbara whispered to Cairn, "God! At least let us get drunk before we start throwing up!"

Moving into the family room, Barbara and Cairn passed Randy Davis and a couple of other guys who were busy slamming shots of tequila. Turning to Barbara, Cairn observed, "If Nicole does let Randy get on top of her it'll probably take her a month to wash all of his puke out of her hair!"

Barbara and Cairn chatted with a few of the other kids as they waited for what they knew would be Nicole's grand entrance into the family room, and a couple of minutes later they saw the other kids parting like the Red Sea as Nicole came over to the bar.

Joining the other Surfer Girls, Nicole said, "I can't for the life of me understand why Tina always invites everyone in the school to her parties."

"Because she's a nice person?" Barbara responded.

"Well I'm a nice person too, but I certainly wouldn't have any ninth graders in my house!"

Randy Davis walked over and barely managed to slur out "Hi, Nicole."

Nicole brightly replied, "Randy! I was hoping you'd be here!"

"Wan some booze?"

Taking the proffered tequila bottle, Nicole turned it up and took several large swallows.

Randy offered, "Wan go out to RV?"

Winking at Barbara and Cairn, Nicole replied, "Sure!"

Randy somehow managed to remain vertical long enough to navigate the 50 feet from the patio door to the RV, and as he and Nicole climbed inside, someone handed them a joint and they each took several hits.

Leaning in close to Nicole, Randy pointed toward the bedroom at the rear of the RV and slur-whispered, "Lesh go back there."

The mixture of pot and tequila had dulled Nicole's few inhibitions and she replied, "Let's go."

As they stepped into the dark bedroom Randy pulled the door shut and asked, "You gone give me ride of my life?"

Thinking, "*What the hell,*" Nicole kicked off her sandals and pulled off her jeans and panties.

After briefly running his hand up between Nicole's legs, Randy began removing his own jeans.

Thanks to Barbara's porno tape, Nicole had at least a rudimentary idea of what she should do, so she lay down on the bed, raised her legs, and spread them wide.

As Randy climbed on top of her, Nicole could see his erect penis in the light that filtered through the curtains. It had looked large while limp in his bathing suit, and while she knew it would be bigger when he got a hard on, what was coming toward Nicole in the moonlight was far larger than she had anticipated. Suddenly, having that thing up inside her wasn't quite as appealing as it might have been.

Randy's cock was resting against the entrance to her vagina when Nicole said, "Randy, wait."

Randy froze, and his face took on a funny expression. Nicole thought, *"Oh my God, he's going to puke on me."*

Randy didn't vomit. Instead, he passed out, and as he collapsed on top of Nicole, geometry and physics came into play and his cock slid all of the way up into Nicole's vagina.

For a moment, Nicole just laid there, almost in a state of shock. Randy's weight was crushing her, and she felt like his cock was going to split her open. Recovered her senses, Nicole rolled Randy's leaden body off hers.

Between the tequila, the pot, and what had just happened, Nicole's head was spinning, and she didn't notice the wetness between her legs as she pulled her clothes back on. Fighting her way through her mental fuzziness, Nicole decided, *"I'll just tell everyone that Randy passed out before we did anything."*

But as she stepped through the patio doors to rejoin the main party, someone gasped and said, "Look, Nicole's got her period!"

Peering down at the front of her white jeans, Nicole could see that the crotch area was literally blood red from the assault of Randy's cock on her intact hymen.

One of Randy's friends laughed and said, "That ain't her fucking period. That's from her giving Randy's old donkey dick the ride of its life!"

Nicole began sobbing, saying "I told him to stop!" That was technically correct. Of course, it was also technically correct that he did stop.

But there was no way Nicole would allow it to pass as just a simple misunderstanding.

CHAPTER 33

The next morning Barbara woke up feeling that there were a whole lot of things about the previous night that just weren't quite right. Before the Surfer Girls had even made it out of Tina's house Nicole was claiming that Randy had raped her.

Barbara had known Randy since they were both in middle school. His father owned a tire and auto repair store, and had done business with Barbara's father at the bank. She and Randy had gone to each other's birthday parties, and had made out a couple of times when they were in eighth grade. In Barbara's book, Randy was a nice guy.

True, Randy had the reputation of being the horniest guy in school, but he also had a reputation of stopping when a girl said, "Stop." But he had been very drunk, and Barbara wondered if he might have let his libido get a little bit out of control.

Barbara harbored no illusions about either Nicole's virtue or her truthfulness. Nicole had been drunk, and the whole school knew about her "ride of his life" comment. Now she was crying "rape", and Barbara felt she needed to find out exactly what had happened before passing judgment.

Barbara called Cairn and arranged to meet her at Tommy's Diner for breakfast, then showered, dressed and headed out the door.

Barbara had just settled into a booth at the café when Cairn came in and sat down, saying, "What's up?"

"Last night with Nicole."

Cairn asked, "What do you mean?"

"Cairn, you know Randy as well as I do. Do you think he would have kept on fucking Nicole if she told him to stop?"

Cairn replied, "How do we know Nicole even told him to stop? She'd already told half the school that she was planning to fuck him last night, and she sure looked like she was going to when they headed out to the RV."

Barbara said, "We're stuck in the middle of all of this. We sort of have to believe Nicole since she's our friend, but I don't think Randy ought to get blamed for something if he didn't do it."

After a brief silence, Barbara asked, "Do you suppose Randy made it to work this morning?"

Cairn replied, "Let's go find out."

Randy worked on Saturdays at his father's tire store, and Cairn and Barbara found him beside the store making an effort to look like he was arranging tires on a rack. The effects of the previous night's drinking were obvious, and the two girls had the distinct feeling Randy was primarily just trying to stay out of his father's eyesight.

Randy sheepishly waved and said, "Hi, Barbara, Cairn."

"Hey, Randy," Barbara replied. "Did you know that Nicole is saying that when ya'll were in the RV she told you to stop and you didn't?"

"Yeah, one of the guys at the party told me she said that. I wish I could swear on a Bible that it wasn't true, but I really don't know."

Cairn asked, "What do you mean?"

"I was drunker than I've ever been in my life! I ain't making excuses, but I really don't know what happened with me and Nicole."

"When we got out to the RV we smoked some pot, then we went back to the bedroom. Nicole took off her pants and lay down on the bed, so I took off my pants and started getting on top of her. I was just about to put it in her and then I guessed I passed out."

Cairn bluntly asked, "Well, did she tell you to stop or not?"

Randy replied, "I honestly don't know."

Barbara asked, "Well, did you fuck her or not?"

Randy said, "We were both in bed with our pants off, but I honestly don't know what we did. I know ya'll have to stick up for Nicole 'cause ya'll are the Surfer Girls and best friends and all that, but I swear that if she told me to stop I didn't hear it, and if we actually did anything I don't know what it was."

Cairn asked, "You swear to God, Randy?"

Randy looked both Barbara and Cairn straight in the eyes and quietly replied, "I swear to God."

The three of them stood there for a minute, then Barbara said, "Randy, we just don't know what to believe right now. But you've always been a good guy, so we'll do a little asking around and see if anybody else knows anything."

"Thanks, that would be cool. If I did something wrong I'll step up and take the blame, but I just want to make sure that I actually did it."

Barbara and Cairn were almost back to the town square when they met up with Chuckie Howard, a boy they had seen at the party.

Chuckie asked, "Ya'll been over talking to Randy?"

Cairn replied, "Yeah."

Chuckie said, "Ya'll think he raped Nicole?"

Barbara said, "We ain't real sure."

Chuckie continued, "Well, I don't know what happened in the bedroom, but I do know that Randy and Nicole weren't in there for more than a minute or so."

"How do you know how long it was?" Barbara asked.

"They finished off the joint I was smoking right before they went back. I rolled another one and I had just lit it up when Nicole came back out."

Cairn asked, "Where was Randy? Did he come out with Nicole?"

Chuckie replied, "No, he didn't. You know Bobo Milton? He was in the RV too, and when Nicole came out Bobo walked into the bedroom to see what was up and said Randy was out cold."

Barbara said, "Thanks, Chuckie. This kind of shit ain't good for either Nicole or Randy, and we just want to find out what really happened before things go too far."

Chuckie said, "I get along with both Randy and Nicole, but I ain't real tight with either one. I know Randy would fuck just about anything that moves, but I also heard what Nicole said about giving him 'the ride of his life' so I ain't real sure what to think either."

Cairn said, "That's kinda where we're at, too."

Barbara asked, "Chuckie, from what you know, who would you believe?"

Chuckie thought a minute, then said, "I'd probably have to go with Randy. It just don't sound like him to rape somebody. But you oughta ask Bobo what he thinks since he was there too."

Barbara asked, "Do you know where we could find him?"

Chuckie said, "He was going to Pine Bluff this morning to pick up a couple of ounces of weed, so he'll probably be out at Mike's Restaurant later trying to sell some of it."

Cairn laughed and said, "Thanks, Chuckie. See you at school."

CHAPTER 34

When the Surfer Girls arrived at school on Monday morning, they found what seemed to be a tacit agreement not to talk or speculate about what had happened between Randy and Nicole at Tina's party, and by the end of the week, the whole incident had simply faded away.

As far as the state of Nicole's virginity went, the whole thing was still up in the air.

Nicole believed that since Randy had raped her, she was still a virgin, at least technically. Therefore, she expected Barbara and Cairn to stick with the Surfer Girls virginity pact.

Of course, a couple of weeks later, when a nice looking guy with a good car and a credit card came along, Nicole dropped her pants in a heartbeat.

And that was the end of the Surfer Girl's virginity pact, not that Barbara and Cairn had considered themselves bound by it in the first place.

CHAPTER 35

Following the witches' tit incident with Bobby Ellis at the pep rally, Barbara had kept boys at arm's length for a couple of months, but she eventually began dating again and had even engaged in a few grope sessions. And despite her worries that everyone would think she was a slut after the Bobby Ellis incident, when she'd said "stop" the boys always had.

Despite the traumatic incident with Bobby, Barbara's interest in sex was still strong, and as she had told Cairn near the end of their sophomore year, when she decided she wanted to get laid, she would.

Two weeks into her junior year of high school, that was exactly what Barbara had done.

CHAPTER 36

Barbara was hanging out in the parking lot of Mike's Restaurant waiting for the other Surfer Girls when Bryan Selig drove up.

Bryan was a college sophomore who was working at the Delta City University library, and Barbara had met him the year before when she was looking for some books that weren't in the high school's library.

Bryan always seemed pleased to see her when she came in, and they gradually developed an easy friendship. A couple of times they had gone out behind the library to share a joint and she'd given him a hug, but that was the extent of their physical contact. When the semester ended Bryan had gone home to Mississippi for the summer, and this was the first time Barbara had seen him since the start of the new school year.

Walking toward his car, Barbara called out, "Bryan!"

"Barbara! I see you survived the summer."

Barbara said, "Barely. Other than a week I spent on the beach at South Padre Island with Nicole and Cairn I was stuck here in Delta City."

Bryan laughed and said, "Bummer, but I didn't even get to go to the beach! My dad made me work."

Barbara put her arms around him and said, "Oh, poor baby." Her tummy was right up against Bryan's crotch, and when she felt a slight stirring in his jeans, she decided, "Why not?"

Ignoring the fact that she had just bought a bag of weed, she whispered to Bryan, "Do you have any pot?"

Bryan laughed and said, "I knew I wasn't getting a hug for nothing!" Lowering his voice, he continued, "I don't have any on me, but I've got some at my apartment. Let me grab some food and I'll run over there and bring you back a joint."

Cairn said, "I don't want to make you do that. I've got my car, why don't I just follow you over to your place?"

Bryan replied, "Cool, I'll run in and get a burger and we'll head over there."

A few minutes later, Barbara pulled her car into a parking spot in front of Bryan's apartment and followed him through the front door.

Bryan walked back to the bedroom while saying, "Sorry to be such a lousy host, but I was going to make a beer run after I ate. All I have to drink is tap water."

Sitting down on one end of the sofa, Barbara replied, "No problem. I wasn't planning on drinking tonight anyway."

Bearing a bag of pot, Bryan came out, sat down on the opposite end of the sofa, and asked, "Did you want me to just roll one for you to take with you, or did you want to smoke one here?"

Barbara replied, "How 'bout if we do one here?"

Bryan quickly rolled a joint and passed it to Barbara, who lit it, took a big hit, then scooted closer to Bryan as she returned it to him.

They talked about this and that as they passed the joint, with Barbara moving a little closer to Bryan each time she handed it back.

The joint finished, Bryan leaned back on the sofa, and Barbara moved in and kissed him deeply.

"Wow!" Bryan exclaimed. "Where did that come from?"

"Even in porno movies people kiss before they fuck."

"Oh. Are we going to fuck?"

Barbara replied, "I hope so. Would it bother you that I'm still a virgin?"

Bryan said, "No, it wouldn't bother me that you're a virgin, but why do you want to fuck me? And why right now?"

"Well, I've been thinking about sex a lot lately, and when I saw you in the parking lot I just decided that I wanted to fuck you. You're nice."

Bryan sat in silence for a moment, then said, "Barbara, right now there's nothing I would rather do than take you to bed. But I do try to be a nice person, and you're a friend, and I wouldn't want to do anything that would hurt you."

He continued, "You remember how I told you about guys ragging on me because I work at the library, and how I tell them, 'I meet a hell of a lot more women in the library than you ever will on the football field!'?"

Barbara replied, "Yeah, I remember that."

"Well I do meet a lot of women, and I sleep with a lot of them, and I enjoy being unattached. Sometimes the first time a girl has sex she wants to make more of it than it is. And right now, I'm not interested in any kind of a relationship. I just want to get high, fuck, and have fun."

Barbara smiled and said, "Bryan, I like you a lot, but I'm not in love with you or anything like that. I don't want you to marry me, I just want you to pop my cherry. After that, you can see me or not see me. Please don't make a big deal out of this because it's really not a big deal to me. I just want to lose my virginity with somebody I feel like I can trust."

Barbara looked straight at Bryan and said, "Let's do this. Roll another joint and we'll smoke it. When we finish, I'll kiss you again like I did before and if you want to take it further we will, otherwise I'll cut out and go back up to Mike's. Okay?"

Fifteen minutes later Bryan became the first of what would be quite a few of Barbara's fuck buddies.

CHAPTER 37

Through her early high school years, Cairn had dated several boys, but other than being a bit grabby, they had been nice guys. A couple of times she had almost convinced herself she was in love, but had quickly gotten over it.

As far as sex went, Cairn wasn't actively pursuing getting laid, nor was she trying to preserve her virginity. She was just waiting for the right boy to come into her life.

While Nicole had begun focusing on boys with money for bed partners, and Barbara was looking only for good sex, Cairn wanted to be in love when she started sleeping with someone. And she had yet to find a boy she could convince herself she was really truly in love with.

Then she met Joey Malone.

CHAPTER 38

All of the Surfer Girls were spending Thanksgiving Day of 1981 with their families. Nicole hoped the sacrifice would pay off with some major Christmas gifts, while Barbara genuinely enjoyed spending time with her parents. And with her fuck buddy Bryan Selig home with his family, she really didn't have much else to do.

For Cairn, it was just another day in the Dumont family soap opera, and she felt duty-bound to take her place on the stage.

Both Cairn and her father had accepted the fact that Lynn Dumont's hold on sanity was continually growing more tenuous. She spent most of her time in the glass-enclosed porch on the rear of the house that she called her studio. She would get up in the morning, load up on the drugs de jour that had been prescribed for her bipolar disorder, then go into her studio to paint. But somehow the colors just never seemed to make the journey from her palette to the canvas.

Thanksgiving Day had started as one of Lynn Dumont's good days. She had taken the turkey from the refrigerator, pulled the stuffing mix out of the pantry, and put some potatoes into a bowl all ready for peeling. Then she had just stood there in the kitchen for nearly an hour.

Cairn and her father had gently eased Lynn out to her studio, and prepared Thanksgiving dinner themselves.

Lynn came to the table for the meal, and Cairn did her best to keep her mother engaged, but by four-thirty she was in tears and her father gently suggested she go for a walk.

An hour later Cairn was sitting on one of the benches on the town square when a young man dressed all in black approached her, saying, "I've got a joint."

Taking the proffered marijuana cigarette, Cairn said, "There is a God."

The young man smiled and said, "Well, maybe, but I'm just plain old Joey Malone. Aren't you that high school chick that's taking some painting classes at Delta City University?"

"Yeah, I'm Cairn Dumont. My best friend's mother is a professor there and she was able to get me into the classes there since they don't have any art classes at the high school. Are you in one of my classes?"

Joey said, "No, my thing is music, but one of my friends paints, and I've seen you a couple of times when I was waiting for him to give me a ride home after class."

Cairn wryly smiled and said, "I didn't think I made that much of an impression on people."

"Oh, it's not like that. I just saw you, that's all."

"Thanks for the fucking ego boost, dude!"

Looking embarrassed, Joey replied, "I'm sorry, sometimes I say some really stupid shit. I just came over here to tell you that there's a party tonight."

"There are a lot of parties every night."

"I mean, there's a party at my house. You could come if you want to."

Cairn asked, "Where's your house?"

Joey replied, "Goth Central Station. Any time after about nine. I've got to go now."

With that, Joey stood up and walked away.

CHAPTER 39

Goth Central Station was a decrepit old two-story brick house about a block south of the town square. James Milton, who had founded Farmers Bank in Delta City two years earlier, built the house in 1926. He committed suicide in 1930 after the bank failed during the Depression, and various members of his family occupied the house for the next forty years.

The last member of the Milton family had died in 1970, and a man from Little Rock bought the house as a place for his son to live while he attended Delta City University. After that, a succession of college students had rented the house.

Joey Malone and three members of his band rented it in September of 1981, when they started college at Delta City University. Joey and his roommates were on the cutting edge of the Goth culture movement, and the house was soon nicknamed "Goth Central Station". It quickly became the hangout for all of the Goth kids in southeast Arkansas, which meant that on a weekend evening there might be as many as 12 to 15 people there.

Cairn wasn't really a Goth kid, but like many young artists, she had adopted an all black wardrobe and one of the few kids at Delta City High School who was aware of Goth culture had dubbed her the "Goth Surfer Girl".

CHAPTER 40

After Joey invited her to the party at Goth Central Station, Cairn called Barbara to see if she wanted to come along. Barbara had declined, saying she was just going to hang out at home. Cairn had not called Nicole, who with her blonde big hair and Dallas chic wardrobe would definitely not fit in.

The front door was open at Goth Central Station when Cairn arrived, so she walked in. Turning to a boy standing in the hall, she asked, "Is Joey here?"

The boy stared at her for a moment, then in an almost incredulous voice yelled, "Hey Joey, there's a girl here asking for you!"

Joey came out of the living room, walked up to Cairn, and said, "Hi. You made it."

In a faux-bored voice Cairn replied, "Well, there aren't a lot of options in Delta City on Thanksgiving night."

Joey said, "Come on, we've got a keg in the kitchen."

As Joey led the way through the crowded living room, Cairn noticed that the partygoers were a mix of holdovers from the punk-rock crowd along with the area's Goth kids, totaling about thirty people. Band equipment filled the dining room, and Cairn asked Joey, "You gonna play tonight?"

"Yeah."

Entering the kitchen, Joey pushed through the group gathered around the beer keg, and after handing Cairn a cup of beer he said, "Let's go out on the back porch and smoke a joint."

As they smoked, Joey asked, "You enjoying the party?"

Cairn replied, "Well, I've been here almost ten minutes and nobody's hit me or puked on me or screamed at me so I guess it's pretty good."

From the back door, someone yelled, "Joey!" and gave a wave indicating that he should come back inside.

Handing Cairn the remainder of the joint, Joey said, "Come inside when you finish it, we're gonna play."

Making her way back to the living room, Cairn saw a girl she recognized and walked over to her, asking, "Aren't you in my art class?"

The girl replied, "Yeah. I've seen some of your stuff, you're really good."

Cairn said, "Thank you. You hang out here much?"

"When I'm really bored I come over here and fuck the bass player, and I come to the parties if I don't have to do my nails or something."

Cairn laughed and said, "I'm a first-timer. I was sitting on the square and Joey came over and invited me."

The other girl laughed and said, "Poor Joey. I'll bet he's invited a hundred girls to these parties and you're probably the only one who's ever shown up."

At that moment, the low droning of a Hammond organ signaled the start of the band's performance, and Cairn turned her attention toward the stage.

The next day Cairn would describe the music to Barbara as sounding like "About an hour and a half of Pink Floyd singing about committing suicide while bombed on downers." But Joey had proved to be a competent if uninspired guitarist, and when he came off stage Cairn had given him a brief hug and said, "Wow! You're really good!"

Appearing shocked by Cairn's hug and words, Joey said, "Let's get a beer and go up to my room."

CHAPTER 41

The décor in Joey's room was typical college boy disarray. The only piece of furniture was a mattress on the floor, so Cairn moved what appeared to be several days' worth of clothes and sat down on it. Joey sat beside her and rolled a joint.

As he passed it to Cairn, he said, "A lot of times girls want to fuck the guys in the band when they finish playing."

Cairn just stared at him, took a hit of the joint, and passed it back.

Taking the hint, Joey asked, "Are you from Delta City? You have kind of an accent from someplace else."

"I was born in Waltham, Massachusetts. I moved here a couple of years ago. Where are you from?"

"I'm from Cleveland. Actually from the suburbs, that's probably why I'm so fucked up."

"How did you get to Delta City?"

Joey replied, "My parents told me I could either go to college or get a real job. My grades weren't very good and Delta City University was about the only school I could get into. But I really just want to be a musician, at least until I kill myself."

Quickly judging that Joey was just talking the Goth talk, Cairn asked, "Well, what if your band becomes really successful, are you still going to kill yourself?"

Joey thought for a moment, and then said, "Well, I'm Goth, so I have to make sure my band doesn't do very well and then I have to kill myself, 'cause if you're really Goth you don't have a future."

Stifling an urge to laugh, Cairn said, "Wow! Your life must have been really shitty. Did your parents beat you or something?"

"No, actually my parents are pretty cool, and I've got a twelve year old brother that I have a lot of fun with. But my dad's an accountant and my mom owns a greeting card store, and they're just so normal. I've always felt like I accidentally got dropped into the wrong family, and when Goth came along it just felt right somehow."

Cairn couldn't help but remember a poster she'd seen from an old James Dean movie where someone says to James Dean's character, "What're you rebelling against, Johnny?" and he replies, "Whaddya got?"

Despite Joey's rebellion for rebellion's sake, Cairn was enjoying talking to him. He was sympathetic as she discussed the situation with her mother, and even admitted, "Wow, and I thought I had it bad!"

Glancing at her watch, Cairn noticed it was almost midnight and said, "Shit! I've got to get home before my parents freak!" She gave Joey a kiss, and when his hand went to her breast she moved to stop him, then let him go ahead and cop a feel.

She stood up and moved toward the door, but Joey just remained sitting on the bed. Cairn thought, "*Prick, you aren't even going to walk me downstairs?*" Then Joey said, "There's not going to be a party, but if you want to come over tomorrow night you can."

As Cairn walked the four blocks back to her house, a police car pulled up next to her and Bigfoot Newton leaned out the window, asking, "Everything okay?"

Smiling, Cairn replied, "Fine."

Walking toward her house, Cairn noticed the police car slowly following her at a discreet distance and smiled. Joey would probably say the cops were harassing him, but she appreciated Bigfoot making sure she got home safely.

Lying in bed, Cairn couldn't get Joey out of her mind and he was in her thoughts as she took her spare pillow and slid it between her legs, pressing it firmly against her crotch.

A few minutes later, she took the pillowcase off and put it on her nightstand. Sometimes her dad did the laundry, and Cairn wanted to make sure she got the pillowcase into the washer before he could notice the wet spot.

CHAPTER 42

The next afternoon the Surfer Girls had gathered on the parking lot at Mike's Restaurant. Nicole went inside to order something to eat, and Cairn breathlessly told Barbara, "I think I'm in love!"

Barbara gave a snort and said, "That's what, the third time this month?"

"No, really. I met this guy last night and we talked and stuff and I really believe it's something special."

"So, do I need to start looking for a bridesmaid dress?"

Cairn said, "No, but do you have any condoms?"

Barbara grinned and said, "Got the hornies bad, huh? I've got some in my purse, but you know you don't have to fall in love with everybody you want to fuck."

"But you talk about Bryan all the time. You must love him."

"No, I love fucking Bryan, but I don't love him. He's just my fuck-buddy. The only reason I talk about him all the time is to keep Nicole from trying to fix me up with some of those dorks at school."

In a petulant voice Cairn said, "Well, I think I love Joey and I think I'm going to fuck him. And that's that!"

Barbara laughed and said, "C'mon, let's get you a condom before Nicole comes back."

CHAPTER 43

That night Cairn fucked Joey and told him she loved him. Joey replied, "Okay."

The next night Cairn fucked Joey and told him she loved him. Joey replied, "Cool."

The night after that, Cairn fucked Joey and told him she loved him. Joey replied, "I guess I kinda love you maybe."

Cairn slept with Joey and told him she loved him through most of December, while he always couched his replies with a large number of qualifiers.

Friday night, December 18, 1981, Cairn had sex with Joey and told him she loved him. He replied, "I love you, too, Cairn."

The next morning Joey went back to Cleveland for the semester break and Cairn never saw him again.

CHAPTER 44

In recent years, the only time her supposed rape by Randy Davis came up was when Nicole got drunk and started feeling sorry for herself, like she was doing tonight as the Surfer Girls finished their last drink at the University Club.

Barbara was pleased with the way the evening had gone. As planned, Cairn had served as the designated jailer, and had kept a close eye on Nicole. Between the two of them, they had managed to present an air of Surfer Girl's normalcy while also making sure that Nicole didn't get out of line.

Then Nicole decided to bring up Randy Davis and the witchcraft thing.

Cairn and Barbara barely managed to muzzle Nicole just before the University Club's bartender came by their table and said, "Okay ladies, finish 'em up, it's time to go."

As the bartender walked away, Nicole started up again, saying, "We killed that guy who tried to rape Cairn. We put a spell on Bobby Ellis and he died. Seeing Randy Davis the other day made me realize how low-life men have fucked up all of our lives. And I think it's time we got even."

After looking around quickly to make sure no one had overheard Nicole, Barbara decided to follow the line of least resistance for the moment and said, "Okay, Nicole, someday we'll get even."

As quickly as they could, Cairn and Barbara got Nicole outside the University Club and into Cairn's car.

Cairn had barely pulled out of the parking lot before Nicole said in a sharp voice, "You're goddamned right we're going to get even, and we're not going to do it someday, we're going to do it tomorrow night.

We already killed two men and got away with it, so I think we can get away with killing a few more."

Trying to calm her down, Barbara said, "Okay, Nicole. We'll get even tomorrow night."

In a voice that was a combination of drunken and conspiratorial, Nicole said, "Shut up, Barbara, I have a plan! Here's what we're going to do. I want each of you to write down the name of a man who deserves to die because of the way he treated you, then we're all going to get together at my house tomorrow night. Cairn, bring all of that witch stuff we got while we were in high school. I know you still have it 'cause I saw it in your attic when I helped you get down your Christmas decorations last year. Then we're going to cast some spells and get rid of those bastards once and for all!"

CHAPTER 45

The next morning Barbara was lying in bed remembering Nicole's words and thinking, "*Whew, Nicole really gets out there sometimes!*" However, despite her best efforts, she couldn't stop thinking about which of the men who had passed through her life she would kill if she could get away with it.

Temporarily pushing thoughts of carnage out of her head, Barbara showered, dressed, and went out to run a few errands. Her cell phone rang once while she was out but Caller ID showed it was Nicole so she ignored it.

When she got home, Barbara found a message on her answering machine.

"Hi, Barbara, it's Nicole. I just wanted to remind you about tonight. Make sure you have a guy's name written down when you come over."

As Barbara erased the message, her phone rang again. Caller ID showed it was Cairn so she answered, "Hi, Cairn. Did Nicole call you too?"

"Yeah, she wanted to remind me to bring the witch stuff tonight."

"Cairn, just between me and you, do you think maybe Nicole is starting to go off the deep end?"

"Hey, Barbara, you're the one who works at a hospital."

"I'm just a little bit worried about her, Cairn. What do you think we ought to do about tonight?"

"Barbara, I'm going to get the witch shit out of my attic and show up at Nicole's with some guy's name on a piece of paper, do some incantations, and hopefully that will get this bullshit out of Nicole's head for a while and we can go back to our regular lives."

"I guess you're right, Cairn. If we play along she'll get over it, and if we don't she'll just keep bitching about it, so we might as well humor her. I'm going to get out my paper and pencil now and think about all of the low-lifes I've known, and I'll see you tonight."

CHAPTER 46

Barbara poured a cup of coffee, sat down at her kitchen table, and began reviewing her life trying to decide who should be the victim of her witchcraft.

It was not an easy task. Barbara didn't dwell on the bad parts of her life, and once she came to terms with her overpowering sex drive, she had always run her own game and very few men ever had the opportunity to do anything bad to her.

She smiled and felt a tingle between her legs as she remembered the night she lost her virginity to Bryan Selig. He certainly wasn't in any danger from the Surfer Girls coven.

Bryan Selig had been her primary sex partner for three years, but just as Bryan had slept with other women, she had also slept with other men.

She had enjoyed them, but it was with Bryan that she really found her sexuality. He was a very good lover, far better than the other men she went to bed with during that period, and had helped her discover all of the pleasure centers her body contained.

With Bryan, it had just been sex, with no real emotional attachment other than friendship, and Barbara learned that while sometimes people wanted to be loved, at other times they just wanted to get laid. Over the years, that lesson had served her well.

Bryan moved back to Mississippi after he graduated, and after that Barbara had slept with few men of varying sexual quality, but no one she felt like having a second go with. And as the years went by, she found plenty of men to fuck, but she never found anyone who could replace Bryan.

CHAPTER 47

Barbara took another sip of coffee and felt the excitement in her crotch grow as she reviewed all of the men she had slept with.

Then she thought of David Henson and the pleasant sensation between her legs fell away.

The incident with David had been during her second year of college at Delta City University, where she was studying nursing.

Barbara was spending Thanksgiving Day with her parents. While passing the mashed potatoes, her mother had asked, "Honey, are you planning to go to Pine Bluff or Monroe tomorrow for some Black Friday shopping?"

Barbara replied, "I hadn't really planned to. Why?"

"We've been using this same old tablecloth for the last ten Thanksgivings, and I thought if you were going shopping you could pick us up a new one at one of the sales."

Barbara thought for a moment, and then said, "Maybe I will run down to Monroe tomorrow. I need some new jeans."

To herself Barbara said, *"New jeans, my ass. What I need is what some guy's got in his jeans."*

Thinking aloud, she said, "Somebody at school mentioned something about this band from Shreveport called 'Cir' playing tomorrow night at the Louisville Lounge. Maybe I'll run down to Monroe early tomorrow morning and go shopping. I can get a room so I won't have to drive home, and go hear the band tomorrow night." After a brief pause, she said, "What the hell, I think I'll just make a weekend of it and come back on Sunday."

Mr. Mason interjected, "Don't say 'hell' at the dinner table, Barbara."

Saying, "Sorry, Dad," Barbara laughed to herself as she thought, *"Would you rather I talked about how many dicks I hope to get in me over the weekend?"*

CHAPTER 48

Barbara was in a great mood as she mingled with the crowd in the Louisville Lounge. Earlier in the day she'd found both the perfect tablecloth for her mother and several nice items of clothing for herself, all on sale. Now the club was packed with lots of cute boys, the band was good, and it had all the makings of a great evening.

"What do you think about the band?"

Barbara turned, saw a guy pointing toward the stage, and replied, "I was just thinking they're pretty good. Have you seen them before?"

"I hang out in Shreveport quite a bit and I've seen them there a few times. By the way, I'm David Henson."

"Cool, I'm Barbara."

Like many other Southern bands, Cir played everything from AC/DC to Hank Williams, and as they finished Bruce Springsteen's "Dancing in the Dark" they smoothly segued into Alabama's "Feels So Right". David moved behind Barbara, put his arms around her waist, and began swaying to the music as he said, "I'm not a real big fan of country music, but this is just a really romantic song."

Moving with him, Barbara thought, "*Romantic, that's good, and he has a decent sense of rhythm. Guys like that are usually pretty good lovers, so David, I think you're going to get lucky tonight!*"

As the song ended, Barbara gently pressed her butt into David's crotch, turned around and quickly kissed him lightly on the lips, and asked, "So, what does a girl have to do to get a beer around here?"

David said, "I'll be right back!"

When he came back with their beers, Barbara led David toward an empty table on the edge of the dance floor.

As they sat down, David asked, "Do you live here in Monroe? I haven't seen you around before."

"No, I live in Delta City, Arkansas. I just came down here to do some shopping and partying this weekend. Do you live here?"

"Yeah, I've got an apartment off North 18th Street. I got a degree in Civil Engineering from Louisiana Tech last year, and I moved here when I got a job." Reaching in his pocket, David pulled out a business card and handed it to Barbara saying, "Just in case you ever need any engineering done."

"Well I don't have a card but if you have a pen I'll give you my number."

Saying, "I don't have one but I'll get one," David got up and walked toward the bar. Returning to the table, he handed Barbara a pen and a cocktail napkin. The napkin bore the Louisville Lounge logo on the front, so Barbara wrote her name and number on the back and handed it to David.

At that moment, an obviously inebriated couple approached the table and David muttered, "Oh shit!" To Barbara he whispered, "That's the guy that gave me a ride over here."

Slurring his words, the other man said, "David, me and, what's your name again? are going to go somewhere and fuck. Can you get a ride home?"

Barbara quickly interjected, "I've got my car. I can give you a ride."

With an abrupt "Okay, bye," David's drunk friend unsteadily led his conquest away.

David and Barbara chatted as they sipped their beers and listened to the music and when their glasses were empty, David asked, "Another?"

"No, that's three for me, and that's my limit when I'm driving. Why don't we go over to your apartment?"

Barbara had discovered that when she wanted sex, she wanted it right then so as soon as she entered David's front door she started pulling off her tee shirt, asking, "Where's the bedroom?"

Ten minutes later Barbara took her mouth off David's still-limp penis and asked, "What the fuck is wrong here?"

David was asking himself the same question. He had slept with quite a few girls in the past, and everything had always worked properly.

Bending back down, Barbara said, "I'll give it five more minutes, but if you don't get a hard-on I'm getting out of here!"

When she raised her head again, Barbara was pissed. In her sexual experience, a couple of drunk guys had barely been able to get a hard-on but she had never encountered one who completely couldn't perform.

Giving David a scornful glance, she said, "Boy, what a rip-off! I was going to fuck your brains out and here you can't even get it up! What's wrong with you?"

David didn't reply. Rage filled his face as he grabbed her, slammed her down on the bed, and punched her twice.

Then he raped her.

When he finished he rolled off and laid there without saying anything.

Barbara got up, pulled on her clothes, and after giving David a look filled with pure hate, she left.

CHAPTER 49

As part of freshman orientation at Delta City University, one of the topics had been "What to do if you are raped". As she drove back to her motel room, Barbara reviewed what she had learned from that session.

Aloud, Barbara said, "Number one, call the police. Number two, do not take a bath or a shower before a rape kit has been done. Number three, immediately contact the nearest rape crisis center or victim's advocate."

In a bitter voice she continued, "Okay, you know what to do, but can you do it?"

Barbara stopped talking but continued thinking as she drove. "*So I call the cops, then what? Everybody in the club could see that I was doing my best to pick up David. And I had been perfectly willing to fuck him.*

"*If I call the cops it's going to be 'he said, she said', and who are the cops going to believe?*"

Glancing in the rear view mirror, she saw that she was getting a black eye and that a thin trickle of blood ran from her lip and down her chin. She thought, "*That would probably be enough to get him for assault and battery.*"

Then her thoughts took a darker turn. "*But this is Monroe, Louisiana. The cops would probably take David's side. And even if they did take me seriously my name and reputation would be dragged through the mud. Do I want my parents to hear about all of the men I've fucked?*"

Back in her motel room, Barbara rolled a joint and sat on the bed as she smoked it. Then she got up and took action.

She always carried a small camera in her purse, so she pulled it out and took several pictures of her black eye and her split lip.

Then she took a shower.

CHAPTER 50

A woman Barbara knew discreetly developed the pictures of her injuries in the photo lab at Delta City University. No one else saw the pictures until she showed them to Cairn later that year, and no one else ever saw them after that.

Barbara managed to hide her injuries with sunglasses and makeup and by the time her face had healed both David Henson and what he had done to her were nothing but rapidly fading memories.

Fading memories, but memories that would never be completely gone.

CHAPTER 51

Barbara put her sex life on hold for the remainder of 1984, and in January, when she started the second semester of her sophomore year, she took her first steps toward becoming the woman she would be for the rest of her life.

One of the elective courses in her nursing program dealt with the physiology and psychology of sex, so Barbara signed up for it and began getting some insights into not only her own sexual behavior, but also what she could realistically expect from the men she slept with.

One of the lectures in that course provided her with what would be both one of her favorite quotes and a very useful piece of information. The topic was male impotence, and the professor had said, "Sexual arousal for a man involves a very complex mixture of both mental and physical stimulation. This mixture is so critical that it is sometimes almost a miracle that a man gets an erection. So, while you might be ready to go at the drop of a trouser, so to speak, your male partner may be at a different point on the arousal curve. However, time can have remarkable curative powers and what might be a total inability to perform one minute might be the best sex you've ever had ten minutes later."

When she finally put David Henson far enough down in her memory to begin having sex again, she tried putting the professor's words into practice and found that by keying-in on her partner she was able to have satisfying sex with almost every man she went to bed with.Nancy Goldberg, a professor from Little Rock, was a guest lecturer for one of the sessions of the physiology and psychology of sex course. She was engaged in research on the newly recognized field of sexual addiction, and gave Barbara a referral to a psychologist named Sharon Dawson, who was assisting her with her research.

Barbara began making a weekly drive to Little Rock to meet with Sharon Dawson, and was gradually able to develop some control mechanisms that at least partially reined-in her more impulsive sexual behavior.

At least most of the time.

CHAPTER 52

As part of her nursing program, Barbara had done clinical work at Delta City General Hospital during her senior year. While she found all of the hospital work interesting, she developed a special interest in physical therapy.

Following her graduation from Delta City University, Barbara moved to Little Rock and enrolled in a two-year physical therapy graduate school program.

She dated some, more frequently had one-night stands, and finally, shortly after the start of her second year, she met Paul Wellington.

Paul started out as a one-night stand that turned into a two-night stand, and progressed to the point where after two weeks he and Barbara were spending every night together.

Barbara hadn't planned to have a long-term relationship, especially this early in her life. She loved sex in great quantities, and love and monogamy just weren't in her current game plan.

But Paul was not only good in bed, his sex drive matched Barbara's perfectly. He was ready and willing anytime she was.

It wasn't all just sex. Paul was the first really intelligent man Barbara had ever been with, and he was also very funny. He frequently amazed her with his depth of knowledge and his humorously twisted views on life.

By the end of October, Barbara was reluctantly admitting that she was in love. She and Paul spent Thanksgiving with her parents, and he presented her with an engagement ring.

Barbara and Paul were married three days before Christmas of 1988 and shortly after New Year's, Paul began a descent into madness.

CHAPTER 53

With Barbara finishing her Master's degree and Paul completing law school they were both extremely busy, and the amount of time they spent in bed began gradually decreasing shortly after their marriage.

Barbara was not happy with this turn of events, but she felt that their sex life would get back to its normal extreme state after they graduated. So she bought a personal shower with a vibrating head and began spending a half-hour or so in the bathroom every evening.

She could tell that Paul was not faring very well. His law school grades continued to be excellent, but he became paranoid that he wasn't doing as well as he should. He started getting upset about the slightest things, and would express his disapproval in a voice that got progressively louder as time went on.

At Barbara's insistence, Paul saw a psychiatrist a couple of times, then stopped going. He started accusing Barbara of wanting to have him committed to a mental institution so she could get rid of him.

Barbara began thinking of divorce, but she hoped that they could hold on and that things would get better after they both graduated.

Then Paul threw the toaster.

CHAPTER 54

Barbara and Paul had overslept, and she was scurrying around the kitchen trying to gulp down a bowl of cereal and a cup of coffee before heading for class.

Paul came into the kitchen, and without a word to Barbara, he put two pieces of bread in the toaster and pushed the start button.

A minute or so later the toaster delivered up two thoroughly burned pieces of bread. Paul stared at the appliance for a few seconds, then picked it up and flung it across the room. It hit the wall a few inches from where Barbara was standing.

Barbara filed for divorce the next morning.

She fought with a feeling that she was abandoning Paul when he really needed her, but she knew that once things took a violent turn, the violence would only escalate.

Barbara had suffered through one violent episode with David Henson, and she had no intention of suffering through another one.

CHAPTER 55

Even though Barbara hadn't intended to get into a long-term relationship, once she married Paul she had begun to construct her dreams around a future with him. And following her divorce, Barbara went through a period where she felt somewhat rudderless.

She buried herself in her classes and focused on finishing her education, and in May of 1989, she received an MS degree in Physical Therapy.

The administrator of Delta City General Hospital was a friend of Barbara's father. Shortly before she graduated, he offered her a very lucrative contract to provide physical therapy services at the hospital five mornings a week and she moved back home to Delta City.

Barbara never knew if Paul had thrown the toaster at her or if he had simply thrown it, just as she never knew exactly what happened to Paul two years after their divorce. No one ever knew if Paul's car had simply stalled while he was crossing a railroad track, or if he had deliberately driven onto the track and turned off the engine.

All anyone ever knew was that the speeding train ended both Paul's life, and the pain that had filled it.

CHAPTER 56

Barbara poured another cup of coffee, returned to the kitchen table, and shed a couple of tears as she thought about Paul. While he had mistreated her for much of their marriage, Paul hadn't been evil, he had just been mentally ill.

She thought, *"Fuck you, Nicole! Why do I have to relive all of this bad shit for the sake of your silly witchcraft games?"*

Barbara quickly ran down what she suddenly realized was a quite long list of men who had passed through her life and her bed, and as she completed her inventory, she concluded that while a few men could have treated her better than they did, only David Henson had actually mistreated her. She picked up the small notepad she used for her grocery list and wrote "Hit List" at the top, and below that she wrote "David Henson".

"What the fuck are you doing?" Barbara asked herself. *"Here you are thinking about killing a man who might have been a total bastard, but who doesn't really deserve to die."*

Aloud she said, "Get a grip Barbara! You've written down the name and tonight you'll go over to Nicole's and do a few chants and cast a few spells that you know aren't real, and then you can all go back to being the Surfer Girls and having fun."

Taking a sip of coffee, Barbara idly wondered who the other Surfer Girls would pick as their victims.

CHAPTER 57

Sitting at her own kitchen table, Nicole was having no problem compiling a list of men to kill. Since she believed almost every man she had ever encountered had mistreated her, her problem would be narrowing it down to just one man.

With so many possible targets, Nicole planned to write down names on a Post-it note as she thought of them, and then pick one from the list.

The first name she wrote was "Randy Davis", the name of the boy she had accused of raping her. But she had mellowed over the years, and unless she was mean drunk she would grudgingly acknowledge to herself that nobody really knew what happened that night, so she scratched out Randy's name.

Then, feeling uncharacteristically charitable, Nicole decided that she would give a pass for everything that happened before she started college since most of the wrongs from that period had just been silly stuff anyway.

Turning her attention to her college years, the first name she wrote down was "Delbert McGraw", her first husband. She then quickly added "Marion Walton", husband number two, and, "Andrew James", husband number three.

CHAPTER 58

Feminism had made some inroads in the South by the time Nicole started college. However, it was a common joke that most of the women who attended Delta City University were pursuing their Mrs. Degree, and so it was with Nicole.

Delta City University was a fertile hunting ground for these wives-in-waiting as it was quite willing to give some kind of degree to just about anyone whose family made a significant financial contribution to the school. A haven for the scions of wealthy families who were either too stupid or too lazy to get a degree from anywhere else, it was truly a target-rich environment for husband-hunters.

When Nicole started college, the Surfer Girls were no longer the social force they had been in high school. Even though Barbara was also going to school at Delta City University, she took her nursing classes very seriously and spent very little time with Nicole. And Cairn, who was attending art school in Houston, didn't return to Delta City very often.

Of course, Nicole soon established a new circle of syncophants who were quite willing to be subservient to her and her ever-ready credit cards, but by her junior year, some of the women in her circle were already engaged, and that simply would not do. No one ever got ahead of Nicole Bailey!

Nicole's dream was to live a life of leisure as the wife of a wealthy husband, and perhaps to be a part of the high society she read about in the Dallas newspapers. And while the moneyed young men she dated at Delta City University were hardly the cream of the crop husband-wise, even they could recognize Nicole's superficiality and had no long-term interest in her.

Trying to expand her hunting area, Nicole began attending various events in Pine Bluff, Monroe, and Greenville, but the local women made it quite clear that the men in their cities belonged to them, and that they would brook no gold-digging interlopers such as Nicole.

During the summer between her junior and senior years in college, Nicole concluded that she wouldn't be finding a suitable husband locally and after giving her situation as much thought as her limited intellect would allow, she decided to just bide her time until she graduated, and then move to Dallas or Houston to resume her husband hunting.

Then Delbert McGraw came onto her radar.

CHAPTER 59

Nicole's father always hosted a barbeque for all of the neighboring farmers and their families shortly after the end of the fall harvest. While Nicole considered any event where she was not the center of attention to be a total waste of time, she always showed up just to lord it over the other females. And there was always the possibility that someone might bring a cousin or friend who might be potential husband material.

At the barbeque held during her senior year in college, Nicole made her usual grand entrance and was immediately livid. The young women who normally awaited her arrival were today surrounding one of the young men at the party, and staring at the group of girls, Nicole soon saw that the object of their attentions was Delbert McGraw.

Delbert was the son of the farmer who owned the land adjacent to her father's, and she had known him since she was a little girl. Delbert was also a senior at Delta City University, pursuing a degree in agriculture. He was nice looking in a country sort of way, and while Delbert's father was not quite as wealthy as Ray Dean Bailey, he was quite well to do, which meant that Delbert also had money.

Nicole would probably have barely acknowledged Delbert's existence on any other occasion, but since he appeared to be the star of the day's show, she intended to share the limelight with him.

Pushing her way through the women surrounding him, Nicole said, "Delbert, how are you?"

Delbert, who knew Nicole and her games well, warily replied, "What's up, Nicole?"

"Just school and stuff. You and me don't get to talk very much so I thought maybe we could hang out for a while this afternoon."

Delbert quickly considered his options. He hadn't really wanted to come to the barbeque, but since his dad and Nicole's father were friends, he had reluctantly agreed to attend.

There were a few cute girls there, but since most of them were in high school, which he personally considered off-limits, he decided to play up to Nicole for a little while, thinking he might at least get a fuck out of the deal.

Taking Nicole's hand, Delbert said, "I know. It seems we're both so busy these days. I'd love to spend some time with you."

Three hours later, Delbert was screwing Nicole's brains out in his apartment near the university.

Shortly before Christmas, Nicole and Delbert had an enormous wedding at her parent's home. For a wedding present, Nicole's father began having a new house built for the newlyweds.

The marriage wasn't exactly a match made in heaven, although both Nicole and Delbert were initially quite happy.

Nicole was happy because if she kept Delbert well fucked he would spend money on her and otherwise pretty much leave her alone, and Delbert was happy because if he spent money on Nicole she would keep him well fucked and pretty much leave him alone.

Nicole's parents were happy because they had always liked Delbert, and most of the other people in Delta City were happy since they also liked Delbert, although they really couldn't figure out why he would marry someone as shallow as Nicole. However, they figured "to each his own" and let it go at that.

Unfortunately, shortly after she and Delbert started their final semester, Nicole found out exactly how well the other students at Delta City University liked her husband. In less than two months, Nicole caught him in bed with four different girls from the college.

Delbert's father provided Nicole with a nice settlement, and the divorce was quiet and discreet.

CHAPTER 60

Following her divorce from Delbert McGraw, Nicole at least tried to give the impression that she was focusing of her studies.

However, with only two months until graduation, even the most determined efforts would have made little difference, not that it really mattered. Ray Dean Bailey's substantial financial contributions to Delta City University had guaranteed that Nicole would receive a degree no matter what.

But since she really didn't have anything else to occupy her time, Nicole played the part of a dedicated student, and in late May received her B.S. in psychology. She really didn't care much about the social sciences, but at that time, obtaining a psychology degree would require the least amount of effort on her part.

Following graduation, Nicole launched into the next phase of her life, which consisted of looking as attractive as possible while spending the summer lying around beside the swimming pool at the Delta City Country Club.

Shortly after the end of summer, construction of the house Nicole's father had given her for a wedding present was complete, and Nicole spent the fall decorating her new home.

But by the time the 1987 holiday season rolled around, Nicole was beginning to chafe at the bit. She was getting bored with Delta City, and she was getting horny.

Unlike Barbara, who simply liked to fuck, and Cairn, who bounced from one semi-serious emotional relationship to another, Nicole generally regarded sex as nothing more than a means to an end.

That end was money. While Nicole could crank up her sexuality when she needed it to get or hold a man, her attitude toward sex generally bordered on indifference. However, she would occasionally get hit by a case of the normal-young-woman-hornies, and they were hitting her now.

So, after a man-less and miserable Christmas, Nicole decided to go to Little Rock for a New Year's Eve charity ball.

CHAPTER 61

New Year's Eve 1987 would be on a Thursday, so Nicole drove to Little Rock Wednesday morning, checked into the same hotel where the charity ball would be held, and went shopping.

Little Rock is the largest city in Arkansas, but it is still in Arkansas. The few people there with at least semi-serious money did their best to put a civilized veneer on their city, but it was indeed a thin veneer.

By no means was Little Rock a party town in the league of Houston or Dallas, nor did it possess those cities style and elegance. But there was a little bit of nightlife, a few nice places to eat and drink, and some quality shopping, so Little Rock wasn't a totally horrible place to live.

Before leaving her hotel, Nicole called all of the stores where she had previously shopped, and even though it was beyond late in the season, a couple of them still had some ball gowns left, and she spent Wednesday afternoon finding one.

Nicole then headed for the nearest package store, as Arkansas liquor outlets are quaintly called, and purchased two cases of various types of liquor, then picked up a variety of mixers in a convenience store, and went back to her hotel.

Nicole had chosen the hotel where the charity ball would be held for two reasons. If she got drunk at the ball, which she fully intended to do, she wouldn't have to drive to get back to her room, and if she met someone interesting at the ball, they could always slip back to her room for a quickie.

Around six o'clock Nicole realized she was hungry and drove to a nearby T.G.I. Friday's where she spent an hour and a half eating and trying to pick up the young man who served her.

The food was good, but her luck wasn't, so she went back to her room to drink, watch TV, and do her nails.

CHAPTER 62

A large crowd filled the hotel ballroom when Nicole made her best grand entrance the next evening. She waved to everyone she recognized, most of whom smiled and returned the wave while muttering, "Oh, shit!" under their breath.

Nicole's position in Little Rock society had been set during her high school and early college years when she had attended cotillion and debutant balls there. Among the other women in Little Rock the feeling was that Nicole drank too much, was a slut, and that she leeched on to any man that she even suspected had money. The men's opinion was more succinct: go to an expensive hooker, you'll get better sex for a lot less money.

But since Ray Dean Bailey was always willing to come up with a fat check for almost any worthy cause, Nicole was at least tolerated in Little Rock.

Nicole studied the room, looking both for potential bed partners and for the nearest bar. There were several banners hanging from the ceiling reading things like "Happy New Year" and "Make it Great in '88", along with some identifying the charity sponsoring the event. Nicole studied those carefully so she could tell people back in Delta City about the ball, although when she did tell somebody in Delta City about the event, she said the charity was working to end prostate cancer in young African girls.

Making her way toward the nearest bar, Nicole passed two nicely dressed men, one of whom she vaguely recognized from high school. Addressing him, Nicole said, "I know you! I heard you'd moved to Little Rock. Didn't you fuck me once in high school?"

With a pained look, the man replied, "I don't think so, Nicole. Let me introduce my boyfriend, David."

The other man gave a tight smile, and Nicole wandered away muttering under her breath, "Great looking queers outside of gay bars is false advertising if you ask me!"

Reaching the bar, Nicole ordered the first of what would be many drinks that evening although it was hardly her first drink of the day as she had been knocking back screwdrivers since noon.

Nicole circled the room, drink in hand, speaking to anyone who didn't see her coming in time to move out of the way and when she emptied her glass, she headed back to the bar for a refill.

When she reached the bar, the bartender was handing a drink to a man of about thirty and almost rudely, she said to the bartender, "Gimme a Jack and Coke."

Smiling at Nicole, the other drinker said, "I've always had a thing for women who really enjoy hard liquor."

Nicole returned the smile, saying, "Far as I'm concerned, when it comes to drinking, there ain't no point in fucking around with those frou-frou umbrella drinks." Extending her hand, she said, "I'm Nicole Bailey, from Delta City."

Taking her hand, the man said, "I'm Marion Walton."

"Like the Wal-Mart Waltons?"

Marion smiled and said, "The same."

Nicole then asked, "Are you from Little Rock?"

"No, I'm from Bentonville, where the Wal-Mart headquarters is."

They engaged in a drunken chat until their glasses were empty, then with dollar signs almost visible in her eyes, Nicole said, "Well, Mr. Marion Walton of Bentonville, I've got a room here at the hotel. Wanna go up there and fuck?"

Portentously, Marion asked, "You got anything to drink up there?"

CHAPTER 63

When Nicole and Marion got to her room, he immediately mixed a drink, and when he finished that one, he made another. He was about halfway through his third drink when Nicole made him put it down long enough to give her a half-hearted fuck.

They spent New Year's Day and the following evening consuming massive amounts of alcohol and engaging in sex whenever Nicole could get Marion to put down his drink long enough to do it.

January 2nd started with Nicole and Marion having room service Bloody Marys for eye-openers, and after downing her second one, Nicole said, "Marion, I hate to break up the party, but I've got to get back to Delta City this afternoon. Problem is I think I'm already too drunk to drive."

Marion said, "Don't worry about it, I'm never too drunk to drive. If you've got a car, I can drive you down to Delta City."

Nicole thought for a moment, then said, "That would be fun. You could spend a couple of days with me in Delta City, and then I could take you up to Pine Bluff where you can rent a car to drive home in."

Raising his glass in a toast, Marion said, "Done!"

Four hours later Nicole and Marion were driving through Pine Bluff on the Martha Mitchell Expressway when Marion's drunken double vision somehow managed to focus on the Pine Bluff Courthouse. Turning to Nicole he said, "Since I'm going to be staying with you in Delta City we could just pull off here and go in the courthouse and get married."

Nicole replied, "Hell, yeah! I ain't been married in ages. Let's do it!"

There is no waiting period for getting married in Arkansas, so the workers in the County Clerk's office are used to requests to wed drunken couples. When Nicole and Marion came in, the employees launched into their practiced speech, trying to get them to postpone their nuptials until they were a little less intoxicated.

Naturally, Nicole started screaming, "My daddy is Ray Dean Bailey and he's the richest man in Delta City and if you don't marry us right this minute I'll make sure all of you get fired."

Deciding that a bitch like Nicole deserved whatever she would get out of a drunk like Marion, the county officials quickly led them through the marriage ritual.

CHAPTER 64

Six months after Nicole's marriage to Marion Walton, Mrs. Bailey invited her daughter to join her for a "girls only" weekend shopping trip to Dallas. Somewhat bored with Marion, Nicole was more than happy to join her.

It had turned out that while Marion was indeed a Walton and he did live in Bentonville, where Wal-Mart's headquarters is located, he wasn't one of the Waltons, and with his meager income he could barely afford to pay the discount chain's "everyday low prices." He had been living off Nicole's money ever since their marriage.

Nicole and her mother had barely pulled out of the driveway for their trip to Dallas when a strange parade pulled in. Leading the way was Ray Dean Bailey, driving an old truck that he used in his farming operation. Behind him was Robert Ross, Mr. Bailey's lawyer, in his Mercedes sedan, and bringing up the rear was Bigfoot Newton, in his Delta City Police car.

Marion was not at all happy as he let the three men into the house. First, he had been sound asleep until Bigfoot Newton's incessant knocking had roused him. Second, since he had been asleep, he had not yet had his first drink of the day, and he preferred not to interact with other people without an alcohol buffer. Third, from the expressions on the other men's faces, Marion was sure they were not just paying him a friendly social call. He briefly considered pouring a drink, then decided that would not be the most prudent course of action and sat down at the kitchen table where the three visitors had gathered.

Nicole's father pulled out a motor vehicle title and placed it on the table, put a set of keys on top of it, then added a large stack of $20 bills. Robert Ross, the attorney, contributed some legal documents to the collection.

Pointing to the papers, Mr. Bailey said in a firm voice, "Marion, this is a petition of divorce. You are going to sign it. In thirty days, your marriage to Nicole will be over. This is not negotiable. After that, Officer Newton will escort you to the county line. Is that clear?"

Marion nodded in affirmation, and Nicole's father continued, "You do get to make one choice." Pointing toward the title and the money, he continued, "This is ten thousand dollars. You can sign the divorce right now and I'll give you the money and sign over the title to the truck outside to you. Then you'll have ten minutes to gather anything that belongs to you, Officer Newton will follow you to the county line, and it will be in your best interest to never come back to Delta City."

Marion nodded again.

Fixing him with a cold stare, Mr. Bailey said, "If you don't wish to take the money and the truck and sign the divorce papers right now, Officer Newton will take you into the bathroom. He'll put you in the tub so you won't get blood all over the place, and when you come out, you will sign the divorce. Then Officer Newton will put you in his patrol car and drive you to way out in the middle of nowhere. As you are getting out of the car, he will accidentally slam the car door on your leg and break it. Then Officer Newton will just leave you there. Am I making myself clear?"

As Marion nodded his head, Nicole's father extended a pen toward him. Marion took it, and with a shaking hand, he signed the divorce petition. He gave a plaintive look toward the bottle of Jack Daniels on the kitchen counter, and Mr. Bailey nodded toward Bigfoot.

As the policeman handed Marion a glass containing two fingers of whiskey, Mr. Bailey signed the title to the truck and passed it to Robert Ross, who notarized it. Pushing the title, keys, and money across the table, Nicole's father said, "Marion, you made a very wise choice. You have ten minutes; you can finish your drink while you pack. Remember, Officer Newton will be watching to make sure you don't take anything that isn't yours."

CHAPTER 65

That afternoon, as Nicole busily tried on the fruits of their $5,000 shopping trip in their Dallas hotel room, Mrs. Bailey broke the news.

"Nicole, I have to tell you something. This morning your father arranged for you to get divorced. Marion won't be there when we get back to Delta City, and he won't be coming back."

A pensive look briefly crossed Nicole's face, then she said, "That's okay. Marion was too drunk to get it up most of the time anyway. Does this blouse look good on me?"

CHAPTER 66

Still trying to decide who should die from her witchcraft, Nicole took a sip of iced tea and began considering her third husband.

She had met Andrew James at a charity function in Dallas early in the summer of 1988. She found him to be attractive, charming, and intelligent, and he seemed to have quite a bit of money.

Nicole's assessment was correct on all counts. Of course, Andrew had some other qualities that weren't readily apparent. He was also a consummate liar, a con man, and a crook. True, he frequently did have quite a bit of money, but rarely did any of it actually belong to him.

Nicole and Andrew's first meeting had been relatively uneventful. She was chatting with some of the other women at the party when she saw Andrew. They exchanged smiles, and a few seconds later, he was standing next to her.

Nicole extended her hand and said, "I don't believe we've met. I'm Nicole Bailey."

Andrew smiled and shook her hand saying, "I'm Andrew James, and I am so pleased to meet you."

Noticing that Nicole was wearing a large diamond engagement ring on her right hand, typically an indication that a woman is divorced, Andrew said, "That's a beautiful ring. Surely no one would divorce a woman as wonderful as you."

Fueled by the champagne she had been drinking like water, she leaned close to Andrew and whispered, "Twice. The first one was a total shit. I gave him all the pussy he could handle and he still fucked around. Then I gave the second one all the money he wanted and he still wouldn't fuck me. All he wanted to do was drink."

Andrew added those little factoids to the mental file he was creating on Nicole, then said, "I'm sorry to hear that. Do you live in Dallas?"

"No, I live in Delta City, Arkansas, but my family supports a number of worthy causes so I'm frequently in Dallas or Houston for these types of events."

Andrew thought, "*Divorced with money. Jackpot!*" He briefly considered making a play for Nicole right then, but rejected the idea. He was already deep into a scheme to relieve some people of their money, and he preferred to work only one con at a time. Also, it appeared that Nicole's money was actually her family's money, and he thought he would have a better chance of making it his money if he did a little planning first.

Pointedly looking at his Rolex watch, Andrew said, "Nicole, you have no idea how much I would love to spend the evening talking with you, but I have a business engagement that I absolutely cannot miss."

Moving closer to Andrew, Nicole said, "Damn, I was hoping you might be willing to keep a poor girl warm in her lonely old hotel room tonight."

Andrew gave her a light kiss on the lips and said, "You have no idea what an attractive offer that is, but I really must go."

Coquettishly Nicole said, "Well if that's the way it has to be."

Thinking on his feet, Andrew said, "But I may have a project in Arkansas coming up in the next few weeks and if you'd care to give me your number I'd be happy to call you if I'm near Delta City."

Nicole replied, "Have you got something to write with? I've had a few drinks and it would probably be better if you wrote it down 'cause you wouldn't be able to read my writing."

Andrew wrote down the phone number, gave Nicole a quick kiss on her forehead, said, "Til we meet again," and began making his way through the crowd.

Nicole thought, "*Damn! I could have used a good fuck tonight,*" and then began checking out all of the other men in the immediate vicinity.

CHAPTER 67

The real name of the man who had introduced himself to Nicole Bailey as "Andrew James" was actually Buford Donaldson, and he was a very busy man for the next couple of weeks.

First, he wrapped up the con he had been working on when he met Nicole, but while that scam had put a couple of hundred thousand dollars in his pocket, he felt it was peanuts compared to what he might be able get in Delta City.

Buford then spent some time researching Nicole Bailey and her family. He found that while Ray Dean Bailey would hardly have qualified as rich by Dallas or Houston standards, he had amassed quite a bit of money from his farming operations and investments. He also learned that Mr. Bailey was well respected in Southeast Arkansas farming circles, and that many of the other farmers in the area looked to him for leadership. Because of this, Buford believed that if he could lure Nicole's father into some sort of scheme, the other farmers would also be quite willing to join in.

From his research, Buford had found that while Nicole was a bit on the shallow side and hardly the brightest bulb on the porch, her father doted on her and would go along with most anything she wanted. So Buford believed that the shortest route to Mr. Bailey's money would probably be through Nicole.

He then turned his attention to coming up with a scheme that would allow him to separate Nicole's father and his friends from their money.

CHAPTER 68

Buford's introduction of himself to Nicole as "Andrew James" had been a spur of the moment decision. Buford had used and reused a variety of aliases in the past, but when he met Nicole, he had used "Andrew James" on a hunch, as it was a totally clean alias. More importantly, it was also a flexible alias, and Buford could construct a variety of different "presents" from the real Andrew James' past.

The real Andrew James had come from Corsicana, Texas, a little bit southeast of Dallas. His father had been a tractor repairman and the family got by, but that was about it.

Andrew was smart, and with the help of scholarships, loans, and whatever jobs he could get he managed to get both a degree in business and an MBA from Southern Methodist University.

Shortly after Andrew's graduation from SMU, an investment firm in Dallas offered him an employment interview, and he invited his parents to ride along with him on the trip.

Andrew James was truly a man with a bright future in front of him as he drove through a freak fog toward Dallas. Unfortunately, a large combine used for harvesting cotton was in front of him, moving slowly in the fog.

Andrew James never had a chance to make a mark on the world. His father and mother had been plain people, of no special note, and were it not for an unscrupulous wrecker driver, the James' family name would have quietly disappeared.

As the wrecker driver was disentangling Andrew's car from the combine, he noticed Andrew's billfold and eased it into his own pocket. A couple of days after that, he spent one evening sweating up the sheets with "that fat girl from the courthouse", and Andrew James' death certificate had mysteriously disappeared from the public records.

Buford, who had previously shared a prison cell with the wrecker driver, gave him $500.00 and a couple of pictures of himself and a few days later, he had a full set of ID's for Andrew James, but bearing his own picture.

And the night Buford met Nicole, Andrew James began to live again.

CHAPTER 69

The last week in June, Buford Donaldson, using the name "Andrew James", drove into Delta City in a new BMW, rented the best apartment he could find, and called Nicole Bailey.

Andrew and Nicole met for lunch at Café on the Square, then spent the afternoon in his apartment engaging in non-stop sex.

Shortly before five o'clock Nicole said, "Andrew, that was so much fun, but I don't think my pussy's ever been this sore. I've got to stop."

Andrew smiled and replied, "Damn, I was just getting started!"

Nicole continued, "Also, I've got some other stuff to do. I'm going to be throwing a little party tomorrow night and I'd really like you to come. My parents and some of their friends will be there, so you'll have a chance to meet a bunch of Delta City people."

Andrew smiled, thought "*Bingo*," and said, "I'd be delighted to attend."

CHAPTER 70

As Andrew pulled into the driveway of Nicole's new home the next evening he smiled broadly because from what he had seen of Delta City, he was sure that Nicole's house was the largest one in town. He was also sure that his instincts were correct, and that pursuing Nicole could be very lucrative.

Nicole greeted Andrew at the door with a quick kiss, then said, "Let me introduce you to my parents."

"Daddy, this is Andrew James, the man I met in Dallas I was telling you about."

A pleasant-looking man extended a work-hardened hand and said, "Mr. James, pleased to make your acquaintance. I'm Ray Dean Bailey, and this is Nicole's mother Merlene."

Saying, "Please, call me Andrew," he smiled at Mrs. Bailey and said, "Well it's certainly obvious where Nicole gets her beauty from!"

As his wife beamed, Nicole's father asked, "So what brings you to Delta City, Andrew?"

With a broad grin, Andrew replied, "Well, I could tell you, but then I'd have to kill you!" Mr. Bailey laughed heartily, and Andrew continued, "Actually I'm here on behalf of the people I work for in Dallas who are considering making an investment in Delta City. I'm doing the preliminary work, but I really can't talk about it much at this point."

Deciding that someone other than herself had occupied the limelight long enough, Nicole took Andrew's arm and said, "You and Daddy can talk business some other time. I've got some other people I want you to meet."

Nicole guided Andrew toward a group of two men and a woman, and from a quick look at their appearance, he knew that they were definitely not farmers.

"Andrew, these are the parents of my two best friends in high school. This is Randy Dumont. He runs those cloth factories south of town."

Laughing, Randy said, "Textile mills, Nicole."

Nicole replied, "Well, whatever. Anyway, Cairn Dumont was one of my two closest high school friends. She's an artist, and she's in Chicago workin' at one of those places that makes beer commercials."

Randy laughed again and said, "Actually, it's an advertising agency." Extending his hand he said, "Pleased to meet you, Andrew. I'm sorry my wife isn't here, but I'm afraid she's under the weather this evening."

Randy discreetly shared a rueful look with the other two people in the group, both of whom knew that Lynn Dumont had now been under the weather for more than five years.

Continuing her introductions, Nicole said, "This is Tom and Katherine Mason. Tom runs that big bank up on the town square, and Katherine tries to teach people how to talk English out at Delta City University."

Katherine Mason laughed and said, "It's 'how to speak English', Nicole, and if you had paid attention in my classes you would know that."

Turning to Andrew, Katherine said, "Actually I'm the head of the English Department at the college," and with a mock glaring look at Nicole she continued, "My field is primarily English literature, however, I also teach a few remedial English classes for students like Nicole who managed to finish high school without acquiring any proficiency in the language."

With a wink at Mrs. Mason, Andrew said, "I'm just plumb tickled as a duck on a June bug to meet you."

Everyone laughed, and Nicole, not quite getting the joke, said, "Barbara Mason was my other best friend in high school. She's up in

Little Rock looking for a place to live while she learns how to fix people's backs and stuff."

Tom Mason smiled and said, "Barbara recently received a degree in nursing, and she's going to do graduate work in physical therapy in Little Rock."

Shaking Tom's hand, Andrew said, "Do you have a business card on you? I'll need to establish some financial relationships in Delta City in the near future, and I prefer to do business with friends, or at least friends of friends."

Tom Mason pulled a business card from his wallet as Nicole whispered, "Some rich people in Dallas sent Andrew to Delta City on a secret mission. But don't ask him about it or he'll have to shoot you!"

Tom handed his card to Andrew while saying, "Despite Nicole's propensity toward gossip, please be assured that we at Delta City Bank are able to handle our business relationships in the strictest of confidence."

Andrew thought, "*Uh-huh. And half the people in the room will be over here asking why you gave me a business card the minute I walk away.*"

In an exasperated tone, Nicole said to Tom, "First Daddy, now you. Can't ya'll wait 'til tomorrow to talk about business? I want to show Andrew my house!"

Taking Andrew's hand, Nicole whispered, "You can meet the rest of these people later," and led him off to tour her home.

CHAPTER 71

As Nicole pointed out various features of her house, Andrew could only think, "*If one of the decorating magazines wanted to do a feature on 'rich redneck chic' this place would be the fucking centerfold.*"

He squeezed Nicole's hand and asked, "Where did you find your decorator, New York, Chicago, L.A.?"

Nicole proudly replied, "Nope! I didn't use a decorator. I did it all myself." Opening a door she continued, "C'mon in here and let me show you my bedroom."

Andrew looked around and thought, "*I see you just moved your high school bedroom intact from your parent's house to here, complete with the stuffed animals!*"

Nicole cut off Andrew's thoughts by grabbing him, sticking her tongue down his throat, and grinding her crotch into his. She said, "Goddamn I'd love to fuck you right now! But there's just too many people around."

Andrew returned the crotch grind and said, "There's always tomorrow night."

Saying, "Yes there is," Nicole pulled Andrew toward an adjacent room where she pointed to an oversized Jacuzzi tub and said, "I had that put in especially for fucking, and I want you to come over tomorrow night and help me try it out."

Andrew said, "I'll be here," gave her hand a quick squeeze, and said, "And now we'd better get back to your guests before they come looking for us!"

CHAPTER 72

As he and Nicole rejoined the rest of the partygoers, Andrew saw exactly what he expected to see. Most of the men at the party had gathered around Nicole's father and Tom Mason, the banker, and their animated conversation ended as soon as Andrew and Nicole made their way toward them.

Looking at her father, Nicole said, "All right now Daddy, ya'll can quit gossiping about Andrew behind his back. I'm going to leave him here while I go talk to Mom and her friends. Ya'll can ask him whatever you want to know about him, but don't ask too much or he'll have to kill you!"

Everyone in the group laughed, and Mr. Bailey sheepishly said, "You know how it is in small towns, Andrew. Anytime a new face shows up everybody wants to know all about them."

Andrew smiled and said, "Well, I have a degree from SMU, but I grew up over in Corsicana, Texas where my daddy worked on tractors before he and my mama got killed in a car wreck."

"I'm sorry to hear that," Mr. Bailey said. "But now that we know a little bit about you, let me introduce you to everybody."

One of the men Andrew met said, "I understand you can't talk about your business, but could you maybe just give us just a hint what you do?"

Andrew's face gave the indication that he was carefully weighing his words, then he began reciting the story he had practiced for a couple of hours earlier in the day.

"My company employs a group of scientists who do research on farming and farm products."

One of the men nodded and said, "Like that stuff they do in the lavatories out at Delta City University."

As a couple of the other men rolled their eyes, Andrew smiled and said, "Something like that."

Continuing, Andrew said, "If the scientists come up with an interesting discovery, we put together a group of investors, and use their money to turn the discovery into a marketable product."

Someone asked, "What kind of discoveries?" and Andrew grinned, asking, "Anybody got a pistol so I can shoot this man? He's asking too many questions!"

As everyone laughed Andrew continued, saying, "Now suppose one of our scientists invents a better shovel. My job is to go out and find a place to locate a shovel factory, build it, and get it up and running."

Everyone laughed again when Nicole's father said, "I got 20 acres I'll be happy to sell you that would be perfect for a shovel factory!"

When the laughter subsided, Mr. Bailey continued, "Seriously, suppose you decided to build a shovel factory here in Delta City. Would any of us local people have a chance to get in on the deal?"

Andrew replied, "Unfortunately, probably not. We generally use our own investor pool in Dallas to finance our projects. Of course, if we decided to make our shovels out of soybeans we'd probably buy a bushel or two from you folks."

One of the farmers said, "And I'd be happy to sell them to you. Do you have a business card?"

Andrew pulled a stack of business cards from his pocket and began passing them out. One of the men read the card aloud, saying, "Lone Star Agricultural Research. Andrew James, Managing Partner."

Andrew grinned and said, "I hope you realize that's just a front company, not the one I actually work for. And the address is one of those places where you rent an office and share a receptionist and a copier and such with a bunch of other business people."

Someone said, "Ya'll sure are secretive!"

Smiling, Andrew replied, "Well, I wouldn't want any of you folks stealing my ideas and running out and starting a shovel factory before I got mine built!"

As everyone laughed, Mr. Bailey said, "I see Nicole coming, and since it's been about 15 minutes since Andrew paid any attention to her, I guess we'll just have to wait 'til another time to do any more talking."

As Nicole pulled Andrew away, Mr. Bailey excused himself, walked into a bathroom, and closed the door. On the back of Andrew's business card he wrote "Corsicana", "SMU", and "parents died in car wreck" and put it in his pocket.

CHAPTER 73

The next day, Nicole's father was sitting outside the Delta City Police Department when Officer Bigfoot Newton arrived to start his patrol shift.

As Mr. Bailey handed over Andrew James's business card, Bigfoot Newton asked, "Is this the fella that's been seeing Nicole?"

Nicole's father nodded in affirmation, and Bigfoot said, "I'll take care of it."

A couple of days later Nicole's father joined Bigfoot for coffee at Café on the Square.

The policeman said, "Mr. Bailey, it appears this Andrew James is on the up-and-up. Everything he told you checked out and I didn't find any criminal record for him, so my guess is he's probably who he claims to be."

Saying, "Thanks, Officer Newton," Nicole's father began to stand up and continued, "Go ahead and finish your coffee, I'll get the check."

Bigfoot took his time drinking his cup of coffee. When he finished, he walked out to his police cruiser. On the seat was a white envelope, and inside the envelope were five $20 bills.

Thinking *"To protect and to serve,"* Bigfoot pulled out of the parking place and began his patrol duties.

CHAPTER 74

Two weeks later they were enjoying a little post-coital bliss in Nicole's "especially for fucking" bathtub when Andrew asked, "What are you doing for the next couple of days?"

Nicole replied, "I hope I'm going to be fucking you. Why?"

"Well, I have to go to Las Vegas for a couple of days and I'd wondered if you'd like to go with me."

"What do you have to do in Vegas, Andrew?"

"Well, I don't really have to do anything, but I just thought we could have a change of scenery, gamble a little bit, and get married."

Nicole idly responded, "That sounds like…did you say 'get married'?"

Forcing his most loving gaze, Andrew asked, "Nicole, will you marry me?"

They made it a quickie since Andrew said he had already purchased the airline tickets, and thirty minutes later they were in Andrew's BMW, headed for the Jackson, Mississippi airport and the last flight of the day to Sin City.

CHAPTER 75

The next afternoon, Andrew actually enjoyed having sex with Nicole for the first time.

As he ejaculated he thought, "*I always knew I'd come into money someday!*"

CHAPTER 76

When Andrew and Nicole returned to Delta City, they settled into a very public marital bliss. They went out to eat almost every night, alternating between Delta City's two sit-down restaurants, and if there was any sort of event in town, they were there acting all lovey-dovey.

In mid-August, Andrew and Nicole attended the Delta City Watermelon Festival and Barbeque on the town square. The only watermelons grown in Delta City were those that a few gardeners raised, but since there really wasn't much to do in Delta City, the town fathers used any excuse they could find to hold some sort of community activity.

Nicole was bustling around doing what Andrew thought of as her "Nicole the princess thing" and he was chatting with some of the farmers he'd met at Nicole's party when he noticed a man staring at Nicole, and with a start realized that he had seen the same man staring at her on several other occasions. Since he was frequently in a position where he might be shadowed by the police agency, Andrew tried to pay close attention to his surroundings and was bothered that he hadn't previously noticed the staring guy.

He asked, "Who's that guy over there that keeps staring at Nicole? I've seen him doing it before."

One of the men glanced in Nicole's direction, laughed, and said, "That's Donnie Taylor. He runs Delta City Appliance World."

Another man interjected, "Back when she was in high school Nicole hung out with a couple of other girls named Barbara and Cairn. I heard Nicole went surfing once and couldn't stop talking about it, so her brother started calling them the Surfer Girls after that Beach Boys song."

The first man said, "Donnie's had the hots for the Surfer Girls ever since high school. He's always following one or the other of them around, but I seriously doubt if any of the girls even know he's alive. But that's all he's ever done, follow them around and stare at them, although I'll bet he's shot 20 gallons of jizz thinking about them while he jerked off!"

Andrew joined in the laughter, while mentally filing the information about Donnie Taylor, along with a reminder to pay a little more attention to the people around him. He could almost smell the money that would soon be coming his way, and he didn't want anyone or anything to screw up his scam.

Deciding it was time to start putting the next part of his con in motion, Andrew said, "I'm probably going to want to get with you boys one night in the next couple of weeks. I've been talking to the people I work for, and there's been a little development ya'll might be interested in."

CHAPTER 77

Nicole's father and some of the other farmers met for coffee almost every morning around ten o'clock at Café on the Square, and a couple of days after the watermelon festival Andrew joined them.

During a lull in the conversation Andrew said, "Ya'll remember how I told you that there probably wouldn't be room for any local people in the deal I'm working on? I still have to clear some of the details with my boss, but there might be a chance for you folks to get at least a little piece of the pie. Do you think we can all meet at mine and Nicole's house on Saturday night?"

Nicole's father said, "Sounds good to me."

Andrew continued, "Invite anybody else you think might be interested, and make sure you bring your checkbooks. If you want to get in on this deal, you'll need to do it that night."

CHAPTER 78

At 6:30 on Saturday night, Andrew was making his final preparations for his meeting with the farmers of Delta City.

He had moved all of the furniture out of the family room, and replaced it with rented folding chairs and an easel with a large paper flip chart on it. There were also boxes of copies that Andrew had personally made at the Kinkos in Monroe so no one else would know their contents. He would give each farmer a stapled stack of pages about a half-inch thick, an amount Andrew knew would discourage them from actually reading them.

Andrew gave Nicole a distracted kiss as she left to spend the evening with her mother, then continued putting a couple of cases of soft drinks in the refrigerator. He knew that it was best not to have people drinking when you were defrauding them. You wanted them stone cold sober, so they would have only their own foolishness to blame for whatever they did. The combination of sobriety and foolishness tended to keep the marks from coming after you when they figured out they had been taken, although Andrew planned to be long gone before that could happen.

CHAPTER 79

By seven o'clock Andrew and Nicole's family room was filled with farmers, along with Tom Mason, president of the Delta City Bank.

Speaking to the group, Andrew said, "Well, let's get started. The minimum each of you can invest is fifty thousand dollars, and the maximum is two-hundred-fifty thousand dollars. After two years, our investors usually make between twelve and fifteen percent on their money."

"Normally, the minimum investment my company will accept is five million dollars. But if you folks can come up with three million dollars between you, I can get you a piece of this deal. If you can't come up with three million, then the deal is off."

Andrew continued, "Tom Mason of the Delta City Bank is here, and he'll tell you exactly how the money part of this thing will be handled."

Tom stood up, smiled at the group, and said, "Basically, Delta City Bank will be serving as an escrow agent. You'll make out your checks to 'Lone Star Agricultural Research'. I'll add them up, and if we have the three million, you'll get a document showing your percentage of the deal. The checks will be deposited in an escrow account at my bank, and if the deal doesn't go through, you'll get your money back after ninety days."

"Next week. Andrew will go to Dallas to take care of the paperwork, and after everything is signed, I'll transfer the money to an account in Dallas."

There was some whispering among the group, then Nicole's father said, "That sounds good to me. Now can we find out what you want us to invest in?"

After quickly distributing the thick booklets of papers, Andrew walked over to the flip chart, pointed to a page reading, "Soybeans, fueling the future", and said, "Quite simply, our scientists have discovered a way to use soybeans as the raw material for creating a fuel very much like gasoline."

One of the farmers said, "I thought someone tried that and couldn't do it."

Andrew quickly replied, "Not just somebody, several somebodys. And you're right, they couldn't make it work. But those somebodys don't have access to the research my company has done."

Continuing, Andrew said, "We didn't figure out a way to totally replace gasoline with a soy product, and that probably can't be done. What we do is start with a quart of gasoline, add three quarts of specially refined soybean oil, then add a little bit of a secret ingredient invented by my company. That gives us one gallon of fuel that will work in any engine that normally runs off of gasoline."

Andrew spent the next hour going through an explanation of the process of turning soybeans into gasoline. When he finished, he said, "I hope all of you were able to follow that. There are parts of it that I don't understand since I'm not a scientist. But I spent a lot of time talking to our researchers and I believe I got most of it right."

Someone in the back said, "I think I got what you were talking about. Course I can't even mix water and a pack of Kool-Aid and end up with something worth drinking."

Andrew joined the laughter, then said, "Okay, now here's how we're going to work this. Tom will be going into the spare bedroom that I use as an office, then each of you will go in there with him for a few minutes. If you want to invest, write a check and give it to Tom. If you don't want to write a check, just chat with him for a minute or so. After everybody's been through my office, Tom will add up the checks and if we have the three million, you fellas will get a piece of the deal. And if we don't have the three million, the whole thing will be off."

Pointing toward the man at one end of the front row, he said, "Why don't you go ahead on in, then we'll just go down the rows."

CHAPTER 80

A half hour later, Tom came out of Andrew's office carrying a stack of checks and whispered to Andrew, "Three million, eight hundred and fifty thousand."

Speaking to the assembled farmers, Andrew said, "Gentlemen, it looks like we have a deal."

CHAPTER 81

Tuesday morning, Andrew called Tom Mason at the Delta City Bank.

"Okay, Tom. We're all ready to go. Nicole and I will be driving to Dallas this afternoon."

Tom asked, "Is everything ready in Dallas?"

Andrew replied, "I talked to the people I work for and they have all of the paperwork prepared. I'll meet with them tomorrow, sign everything, and fax a copy to you. Then you can transfer the money to Dallas. I don't foresee any problems."

Hanging up the phone, Andrew smiled and thought, "*No, there won't be any problems. I made up the paperwork a month ago, it's in the trunk of my car, and by this time tomorrow all of that money will be all mine!*"

CHAPTER 82

That night, as Andrew drifted off to sleep in their Dallas hotel room, he glanced at Nicole and thought, *"That's the last time I'll ever have to stick my dick in your moron cunt."*

Nicole was still asleep as Andrew prepared to leave the next morning, so he gave her a kiss and said, "After I finish my business stuff I'll come back and pick you up and we can have a nice lunch before we head back to Delta City."

Nicole mumbled, "Okay. I love you."

When Andrew reached his rented office, he took the papers from his car trunk and faxed them to Tom Mason at the Delta City Bank.

Ten minutes later Andrew called the bank, asking, "Did the paperwork come through okay, Tom?"

The banker replied, "Sure did. I've got Robert Ross checking it to make sure it's all right legally." At that moment a voice in the background said, "It looks good to me, Tom."

Tom said, "Hang on for just a minute and I'll transfer the funds to your Dallas bank." A few seconds later he said, "The money should be in your account now, Andrew."

"Okay, I'll give them a call and make sure it came through, then I'll pick up Nicole and head back to Delta City. I'll come by and chat with you in the morning."

Andrew called his Dallas bank, and after making sure that the funds had come through from Delta City, he immediately transferred the money to his secret bank account in the Cayman Islands.

Then, he drove to the airport where he bought single plane tickets to New York, Miami, Las Vegas, and Los Angeles on four different airlines. He spread the tickets face down on a bench, closed his eyes, and let his hand drop on one of the tickets.

Andrew turned the ticket over and saw the ticket he had picked was for Las Vegas. He then circulated through the airport, telling people he had tickets he couldn't use, and soon gave the other three away.

Inside of the next half hour, passengers carrying plane tickets in the name of "Andrew James" departed for four different cities.

CHAPTER 83

Aloud, Nicole said "motherfucker" as she remembered her marriage to Andrew James.

After Andrew ran out on her, there was a lot of ill feeling toward Nicole in Delta City. Quite a few of the farmers felt they would still have their money if she hadn't brought a con man into their midst. But as word got around that Nicole's father had made and lost the $250,000 maximum investment, feelings gradually began to soften.

Mr. Bailey had done his best to locate Andrew by spreading several hundred-dollar bills around the Delta City Police Department and hiring a private detective from Dallas. But the trail went cold in New York, Miami, Las Vegas, and Los Angeles and nobody could pick up Andrew's trail after that.

Mr. Bailey had ordered Nicole to keep a low profile during the period when she was on every shit list in Delta City, and the only time he allowed her to leave the city limits was when she flew to Mexico with her mother to get divorced from Andrew.

CHAPTER 84

Nicole took a sip of her iced tea, drew a circle around "Andrew James" on the Post-it note, and said, "Motherfucker, you're going to die!"

The name selected, she decided to make a run to Piggly Wiggly to pick up a few things for the evening. Even though tonight's gathering would only include the other Surfer Girls, Nicole was always a good hostess.

CHAPTER 85

Cairn was sitting at the breakfast bar in her kitchen trying to decide which of the men who had passed through her life she thought should die. She was pretty sure it would be someone from her Chicago days, but she wanted to make sure she considered all of the possibilities.

And Cairn wanted to make sure that whoever she chose really deserved to die, because she had a secret she had never shared with any of the other Surfer Girls.

When Nicole got drunk, she would claim that the Surfer Girls had killed Bobby Ellis with their witchcraft, but Cairn knew she really didn't believe it. Barbara had thought the whole witch thing had just been a silly game, and that Nicole's tit-flash had distracted Bobby just before he pulled out in front of the truck that hit him.

But unlike any of the others at Mike's Restaurant that fateful day, Cairn had been looking directly at Bobby as she chanted the incantation, and had seen his body stiffen as he frantically pressed the brake pedal to keep his car from moving. She also had heard him scream as some unseen force pushed Bobby's car in front of the fast-moving truck.

In the years since, Cairn had seen and heard many other things that supported the possibility that supernatural acts might be a part of everyday life. So, while she wasn't prepared to state unequivocally that witchcraft was real, neither was she willing to discount it totally. And just in case tonight's gathering of the Surfer Girl's coven accomplished its aims, Cairn wanted to make sure that whoever she chose would deserve whatever fate he might meet.

CHAPTER 86

What she would later refer to as her "Joey thing" would become the template for Cairn's relationships with men.

Ironically, during her final year of art school Cairn ran into the drummer from Joey's band. He told her that Joey now got up every morning, put on a suit, and went out and sold real estate. He said Joey had a beautiful little girl, a pregnant wife, and a house in the suburbs, and seemed very happy.

Somehow, Cairn was not surprised.

But just as it had been with Joey, through the remainder of her life Cairn would meet a man she wanted to sleep with, then convince herself she was in love with him before going to bed with him.

The only break in this pattern was the year she spent in Chicago.

CHAPTER 87

Nineteen eighty-six was a wonderful time for a twenty-one year old woman to be starting her career in Chicago, and Cairn had begun that fateful year with high hopes. After her three years of art school in Houston, a prestigious Chicago advertising agency had hired her as a graphic artist. Cairn assuaged any guilt about selling out by rationalizing that the job would allow her to earn a living in the field she loved while she developed a clientele for her fine art works.

Nineteen eighty-six was also a big year for cocaine in Chicago and the white powder soon became a large part of Cairn's life.

She smoked pot all through high school, experimented with magic mushrooms, and had done cocaine a couple of times in Houston, although it had not really been a drug of choice for her.

But things changed when she moved to Chicago.

Everybody at the advertising agency worked long hours, and to keep going, many of them turned to cocaine. Lower-level workers would close their office doors to do a quick line, while upper management didn't even bother with the doors, sometimes even putting phone calls on hold to take the drug.

Cairn received a decent salary, but it was nowhere near enough to pay for all of the cocaine she was consuming, and like many other young women at that time, she began spending most of her free time with men who had enough money to support her habit.

As had many other users, Cairn soon discovered that one of the effects of doing cocaine is that it makes you want to do more cocaine, and Cairn was having sex with more and more men in order to do more and more cocaine.

In what were becoming her fewer and fewer lucid moments, Cairn considered that having sex with men just because they gave her cocaine was not much different from ordinary prostitution. But, like many others, she rationalized that giving up a piece of ass in exchange for a couple of hundred buck's worth of cocaine wasn't much different than putting out following a two-hundred dollar dinner.

But the game changed substantially when Cairn met Jared DeCosta.

CHAPTER 88

If you went far enough up the food chain, Jared DeCosta was technically Cairn's boss. He was the head of the creative department at the advertising agency, but he really didn't have too much contact with the employees at Cairn's level.

That changed one night when Cairn went to one of the Rush Street bars after work. Ostensibly, she was just going out for a drink with a couple of people from the office, but what Cairn really planned to do was to get with one of the hard-partying men with deep pockets who were a fixture on Rush Street.

As Cairn walked into the bar, Linda Devinie, one of the other women in her group, waved to someone on the other side of the room. She turned to Cairn and asked, "Have you met Jared DeCosta yet? He's the boss of our department."

Cairn replied, "No, I've seen him a couple of times, but I've never spoken to him."

Taking Cairn's arm, Linda said, "Come on, I'll introduce you."

Jared DeCosta was sitting at a table by himself. He stood when the two women approached.

"Mr. DeCosta, this is Cairn Dumont. She joined the creative department last September."

"Cairn, so nice to meet you. I hope you're enjoying working with us."

Before Cairn could respond, Linda Devinie said, "Please excuse me, I really have to go to the ladies room. I'll catch up to you later."

Cairn briefly smiled at Linda, then returned her attention to the man, saying, "Mr. DeCosta. I'm really pleased to meet you."

"Please, call me Jared. And since you seem to have been abandoned, why don't you join me for a few minutes so I can get to know you?"

Cairn quickly looked around the room as she considered Jared's offer. She really wanted some cocaine, but none of the partying crowd seemed to be there. She decided she would sit with Jared for a few minutes, then excuse herself and pursue her own interests.

Taking a seat, Cairn said, "Thank you, Jared. I'm meeting someone, but I'd love to talk to you until they get here."

Jared replied, "That will be fun." He slid his hand down Cairn's leg under the table, then said, "Perhaps I know your friend," as he pressed something into her hand.

Cairn took a furtive glance at what Jared had given her and recognized the small plastic bag filled with white powder.

Jared continued, "Why don't you go to the ladies room and I'll have a drink waiting when you come back."

In the restroom, Cairn found a vacant stall and dug out some of the cocaine with her apartment key. She quickly inhaled, then repeated the process with the other nostril. Then she stood there for a few moments trying to collect her thoughts.

Around the office, Jared DeCosta seemed pretty much a straight arrow. He lived in an expensive home on the North Shore with the wife he had married while they were in college and two teen-aged children. It was common knowledge around the office who did and did not indulge in the white powder, and Jared was not known as an indulger.

She studied the bag of cocaine in her hand and thought, "*That's a lot of fucking coke!*" Sniffing, she thought, "*Good shit, too.*" She snorted a little bit more of it and returned to the table where Jared was waiting.

As Cairn sat back down she tried to put the bag of coke back in Jared's hand, but he whispered, "No, you keep it. There's plenty more where that came from."

Cairn and Jared made small talk as they enjoyed a couple of drinks, and both of them made several trips to the restrooms.

They were just finishing their drinks when Jared said, "Cairn, I'm going to need to promote someone to be the creative team lead on the beer account. I know you haven't been with us very long, but I've seen your work and it's quite good. Do you think you might be interested in becoming a team lead?"

Cairn sat for a moment to make sure that the words had correctly penetrated the booze and cocaine, and then said, "Jared, I would love to discuss it with you."

Jared smiled and said, "With all the noise, I'm afraid serious conversation would be impossible here. However, I keep a small apartment a couple of blocks away here for when I work too late to go home to the suburbs. And I have several more of those little plastic bags there."

Cairn was somewhat shocked by what Jared had said. To her, it had a ring of "party with me and you'll get promoted". She had always regarded women who fucked their way to the top with disdain, and had vowed that she would never do that.

But, Jared had intimated that he had more cocaine at his apartment, and Cairn well knew that the quid pro quo under these circumstances usually lay between her legs, or in what she could do with her mouth.

The booze and coke made the rationalization easy for Cairn. She had come in the bar planning to fuck some guy who would provide her with coke. She could fuck Jared and get coke, and might even get a promotion.

She squeezed Jared's leg under the table and said, "Let's go!"

CHAPTER 89

Outside the bar, Jared hailed a cab for the ride to his apartment and once inside the taxi, he said, "Yes, Cairn, I've heard very good things about you and your work."

"Thank you, Jared. I didn't know you were even aware of me."

"Cairn, you don't get to be the creative head at a major advertising agency without paying attention to details. In all honesty, I don't know everyone who works for me by name, but I get monthly reports on all of the members of the creative department, and I review all of the work they produce."

Cairn ruefully said, "Oh God. I hope you didn't see some of the stuff I did during my first month or so. It was total crap!"

Jared laughed, saying, "And I'm glad you'll never see the work I did during my early days in the business. Actually, I pay close attention to new employees' first work. It provides a basis for judging their progress. And Cairn, you are progressing quite well."

Cairn smiled and said, "Thank you."

"I've also heard other good things about you, Cairn. Your manager told me that you are very organized and have natural leadership skills, and these are the qualities I look for in team leaders."

Jared's comment puzzled Cairn as she considered one of her great failings to be her complete lack of organization, both at work and in her personal life. And not only was she not a leader, she wasn't much of a follower either. She had always just kind of done her own thing. But she wasn't about to argue with a man who was going to give her cocaine and who could give her a promotion.

"And here we are," Jared said as the cab pulled up in front of a high-rise apartment building on Lake Shore Drive.

CHAPTER 90

Cairn noticed that the apartment was nicely but sparsely furnished, but then Jared had said he only used it when he had to work late.

Pointing toward the kitchen, Jared said, "Why don't you mix us a drink and I'll be right back," then walked into the bedroom and closed the door.

Cairn walked out into the living room, set the drinks on the coffee table, and sat down on the sofa just as Jared returned from the bedroom. He had changed from his suit into a bathrobe, and he sat down next to Cairn on the sofa.

Pulling out a bag of cocaine, Jared smiled and said, "I move that we postpone our discussion of the team leader position until another time."

Cairn smiled and said, "No problem."

Jared took a sip of his drink, poured some of the coke on the coffee table, and handed Cairn a rolled up dollar bill. Cairn inhaled some of the drug, and then passed the dollar bill back to Jared.

Jared bent over the table and did some coke, then sat back on the sofa. Giving Cairn a pointed look, he said, "I assume you know how the game is played," and opened the robe to reveal his erect penis.

Cairn took a sip of her drink, snorted a little more cocaine, and then dropped to her knees in front of Jared.

They continued doing coke and engaging in various forms of sexual activity until nearly four o'clock in the morning when they inhaled the last of the cocaine and Jared said, "I have an early meeting so we'd better call it a night."

Cairn watched as Jared walked into the bedroom, returned with a $20 dollar bill, and extended it toward Cairn saying, "I hope you won't mind getting your own cab, I really need to crash now."

CHAPTER 91

When Cairn arrived at her desk the next morning, she found a memo advising her there would be a meeting of the entire creative group at four that afternoon.

As she was walking to the conference room Cairn saw Linda Devinie and asked, "Any idea what this meeting is about?"

Linda laughed and said, "It's either something extremely important or somebody just noticed we hadn't had a department-wide meeting in a while and got a wild hair up their ass!"

Cairn said, "It's the first one they've had since I've been here and I've got one hell of a headache so I hope it's not a big deal."

Linda laughed and said, "So you and Jared had a good time, huh?"

Cairn just smiled.

When she entered the conference room she saw Jared DeCosta at the head of the table, talking to another man she semi-recognized, and asked Linda, "Who is that Jared is talking to?"

Linda replied, "Walt McGuire, he's the senior vice president of the creative department and Jared's right-hand man."

Jared stood and said, "Hello, and thank you all for coming. Some of you may be aware that the creative department in the New York office has not been performing as well as senior management would like."

A couple of people nodded their heads in affirmation, and Jared continued, "A couple of months ago I began having tentative talks with the New York management about taking over their creative department."

There was a small buzz of whispers but Jared ignored it and kept speaking. "Two weeks ago, we reached an agreement for me to move to New York and take over the creative department there."

The whispering increased and Jared said, "Please hold your discussion until I finish my announcement. For various reasons it was decided to keep this change of command secret. Right now the head of creative in New York is being informed that I will be replacing him, and after this meeting I will be flying to New York to take over their operation tomorrow morning. This will be my last day here in Chicago."

The whispering resumed with greater intensity, and Jared let it go on for a minute or so.

Cairn was in a state of shock and she just stared at Jared. To Linda she whispered, "That son-of-a-bitch! Last night he was talking about promoting me and all the time he knew he would be leaving the office after today."

Jared began speaking again, saying, "I'm sure most of you are wondering who will be my replacement here in Chicago. Allow me to present Walt McGuire, who will be taking over creative. He has a few words for you."

As Jared sat down Walt stood up and said, "While I really hate to see Jared go to New York I have to admit that I am thrilled to be taking over here. Why don't we give Jared a big hand?"

As the applause began Cairn thought, *"A big hand my ass! What I'd really like to give that bastard is the finger."*

Walt began speaking again, assuring everyone there would be no major changes in the department, and Cairn tuned him out as she whispered to Linda, "That motherfucker! I'd have fucked him just for the coke! He didn't have to throw out that team lead shit just to get my pants off!"

As the meeting began to break up, Cairn made her way through the crowd until she was almost in Jared's face, forced a smile, and said, "Congratulations on your new position, Jared."

Jared returned the smile and said, "Thank you. I don't think we've met, but I've seen you around the creative department. Good luck in your career."

Cairn was livid. Not only had he fed her a line of shit last night, today he acted like he didn't even know her, so she leaned in close and almost hissed, "You may not remember me, but I damn sure remember sucking your cock last night!"

Jared gave a start of recognition, then smiled and turned to another of the well-wishers.

While she didn't yet know it, Cairn's encounter with Jared would prove to be a pivotal point in her life.

CHAPTER 92

When she left the meeting, Cairn went out and got on the CTA bus that would take her home. She was soon deep in thought as the bus bounced along.

She thought, *"Cairn, what in the hell has happened to you? You're nothing but a coke whore. It was bad enough when you were just fucking guys who would get you high, but falling for the shit Jared was feeding you last night is just too much.*

"This could be your last chance, kid. A couple of more years and you'll be nothing more than another burned-out bitch. It's time for some major changes."

When she reached her apartment, Cairn threw a few clothes in a bag then went out and hailed a cab to take her to O'Hare Airport.

She wandered around the airport terminal for a while trying to decide where she wanted to go. She didn't have a particular destination in mind, Cairn she knew she had to get out of Chicago right now and get her life straightened out.

In one of the airport stores, she spent a few minutes staring at a row of beer glasses with the names of various locations printed on them, then noticed one that said, "Welcome to New Mexico". She frantically dug through her purse until she found her address book, then flipped through it looking for a name.

Sue Christiansen was a girl Cairn had gone to art school with. After graduation, Sue had moved to New Mexico to try to make a living in the thriving art scene there. Cairn looked up her number and went in search of a pay phone. A couple of hours later she was on a plane to Taos, New Mexico.

CHAPTER 93

Saying, "Nicole, sometimes you are such a cunt!" Cairn walked to the refrigerator, pulled out a bottle of water, and returned to the breakfast bar.

She had managed to totally bury her Chicago year in her mind, and if it weren't for Nicole's silly-ass witchcraft games she wouldn't be thinking about it now.

The possibility that the witchcraft might actually work also troubled her. Deep down Cairn knew that the only man she had ever known who really and truly deserved to die was already dead and lying stiff as a board in the freezer in her backyard shed.

She also knew that had it not been for Jared DeCosta's despicable actions she would probably still be toiling in some cubicle at some advertising agency, instead of living the life she now mostly enjoyed.

After her rapid departure from Chicago, Cairn had spent the next few months in Taos crashing with Sue Christiansen, her friend from art school. Sue did brass sculpture, and while she wasn't getting rich, she had developed a following among the devotees of Taos art.

Cairn's parents did not know how she had been spending her time in Chicago, but when she called them, they kept the questions to a minimum.

"Dad, I hope you can understand that there are some things I don't want to talk about right now, but I really felt I had to get out of Chicago when I did."

Her father replied, "Cairn, most of the time your judgment has been pretty good. I'm willing to believe that a total change in your life was necessary and a good thing."

"Thanks Dad. I need a really big favor from you."

Mr. Dumont laughed and said, "How much?" Then deciding that his comment might be too flip under the circumstances, he continued, "Sorry Cairn, I was just trying to make a joke. What do you need from me?"

"Dad, when I decided to leave Chicago I just got up and left and I really don't want to go back there, but everything I own is still in my apartment. Do you think you could fly up there and close up the place?"

"Can it wait until next weekend, Cairn? I'm pretty swamped at work right now."

"No problem. My rent is paid through the end of the month and I'll call my landlord and let him know you'll be coming up. What I'd like you to do is ship all of my art stuff and my finished pictures to me. I really don't care about the furniture and other shit, but I'm going to see if I can sell some of my work here in Taos."

Her father replied, "Don't say 'shit' Cairn," then cringed as the words left his mouth.

But Cairn just laughed and said, "I love you, Dad."

When the pictures arrived in Taos, Cairn took them to the gallery that handled Sue Christiansen's work. The gallery owner agreed to show some of Cairn's pictures, and they sold quickly. Cairn started painting again and her pictures sold as fast as she could finish them.

Sue Christiansen provided her with a non-judgmental shoulder to cry on, and it wasn't long before Cairn's time in Chicago faded into the realm of bad memories.

Cairn spent the next year and a half in Taos, making a very good living from her painting.

Then came the phone call.

It was from Harry Laird, the Delta City chief of police. Cairn's parents had been returning from dinner the previous evening when a freak tornado hit their car.

Returning to Delta City for the funeral, Cairn's intent was to put her parent's house on the market and return to Taos.

Barbara and Nicole had been at the funeral, and after making sure that Nicole was out of earshot, Cairn invited Barbara to come over for a "good-old-days drunk."

CHAPTER 94

After the funeral, Cairn and Barbara were sitting at the kitchen table slowly sipping Jack Daniels and Coke. Looking around the room Cairn said, "I try not to, but I can't help but think of this as the place where Dad and I lived and Mom existed."

Barbara patted her hand and said, "It's funny, but when people talked about the Surfer Girls, Nicole was always the leader, I was always the strong one, and you were the spacy one. But knowing what you had to go through with your mother I think it was probably you who was the strongest of all of us."

Picking up a tissue, Cairn wiped her eyes, and said, "I know it wasn't Mom's fault, but that didn't make it any easier to live with."

Barbara pointed toward the blank canvas that still stood in Lynn Dumont's studio, and said, "I always thought that empty canvas was kind of a metaphor for your mother's life. It had been started, but it would never be finished. It would always be in kind of a holding pattern."

Cairn smiled and said, "You know, Barbara, somehow you always know just what to say."

"Why don't you finish it?"

Cairn replied, "Okay, turned up her glass, and drained the rest of her drink."

Barbara laughed and said, "Not the drink, dumbass, the painting. Why don't you paint something on your mother's blank canvas? It might give you a sense of closure."

Cairn gave a wan smile, then kept the talk focused on the Surfer Girls' high school days as she and Barbara emptied the bottle of Jack Daniels.

CHAPTER 95

The next morning Cairn visited the office of Robert Ross, her father's attorney.

After giving her a copy of her parent's wills, he told her what she would inherit. There was the house and her father's car, some investments he had made, and life insurance proceeds. She would not be rich, but if she chose to, she could live comfortably in Delta City with nothing more than her inheritance.

But Cairn had zero interest in living in Delta City and asked Robert Ross to handle any matters necessary to sell the house.

Then she went back to what had once been her home to begin purging it of whatever she didn't want to sell or keep.

She puttered around looking in closets, picking things up and putting them down, and after an hour of accomplishing nothing she finally succumbed to a pull she had been feeling every since she returned to the house.

She walked out to the glassed-in back porch that her mother had used for a studio, and sat down in front of the blank canvas that had been patiently perched on an easel for so many years.

She felt frozen in space and time, and shed a few tears as she thought of all the years her mother had been trapped inside her mental illness. Then she put some colors on her mother's palette, picked up a brush, and began to paint.

After four hours of intense work, Cairn stopped. As she stared at her mother's once-blank canvas, she saw the beginnings of what she knew would be the finest picture she would ever paint.

She called Robert Ross and told him she had decided not to sell the house.

The Surfer Girls would be together again in Delta City.

CHAPTER 96

Cairn turned around on her stool and looked at the painting she had created on her mother's blank canvas, which now hung in her great room. She knew she could have sold it for four or five times the amount she usually received for her work, but she also knew that she would never part with it for any amount of money. While the painting had sprung from her talent, she had created it on a foundation prepared by her mother and it would not be for sale as long as Cairn was alive.

Still lost in the thoughts of her past, she idly thumbed through some of the junk mail that had been piling up on her breakfast bar.

Picking up a fake credit card from the junk mail pile, along its edge she saw the traces of white powder where Terry Harding had used it to make lines of cocaine that fatal night.

Taking the credit card to the sink, she rinsed off the cocaine, and threw the card into the trash. Walking back to the breakfast bar, she picked up a notepad and wrote "Jared DeCosta".

She remembered the night in Jared DeCosta's apartment when he had taken out his cock and said, "I assume you know how the game is played."

Cairn did indeed know how the game was played, and had no problem with fucking men who gave her cocaine. But throwing in the possibility of gaining position, power, or money made it a completely different ballgame.

She rationalized that if Jared DeCosta didn't deserve to die, the witchcraft would fail, and if the witchcraft did work, she would not feel especially guilty if Jared DeCosta lost his life.

Walking into the hallway, Cairn pulled down the hidden stairs that led to the attic and began gathering up the Surfer Girls spell-casting gear.

CHAPTER 97

As the Surfer Girls were deciding whom to kill with their witchcraft, Dan Arthur Truman was having a cup of coffee and talking to Donnie Taylor at Café on the Square.

Donnie was sitting at the counter in the crowded restaurant, and he had momentarily cringed when Dan Arthur came in and sat down next to him.

Knowing he had been a little bit rough on Donnie when questioning him about the stolen Mercedes, Dan Arthur wanted to try to smooth things over so he laughed and put his hands in the air, saying, "No uniform, no badge, Donnie, I just came in for a cup of coffee. You don't even have to talk to me if you don't want to."

Donnie smiled and said, "No problem, Dan Arthur. You were just doing your job. But I tell you, I was about ready to confess to sinking the Titanic before you got through with me!"

"Well, at least you know the taxpayers are getting their money's worth out of me."

Donnie said, "Speaking of getting your money's worth, I'm going to the appliance and electronics shows next week."

"Shows?"

"Every year the manufacturers throw big shows where they display all of their newest products for their dealers to see. I go and order the stuff I'll have in the store for Christmas shopping."

"I always figured you just had some catalogs you ordered from."

"That's the way I order during most of the year, but the shows give us a chance to talk to the manufacturers and get an idea of what they're going to be pushing over the holidays. They give us some free meals and a few drinks, and I get to write the whole thing off on my taxes!"

"Maybe I should get into your business, Donnie. I'm lucky if the city gives me a paycheck to pay taxes on."

Laughing, Donnie said, "Anyway, Sunday I'll drive down to Monroe and spend the night, then catch an early flight to Chicago on Monday for the appliance show. Monday night I'll fly out to Las Vegas and spend Tuesday at the electronics show."

Dan Arthur said, "Sounds like you'll be cramming a lot into not much time. Are the shows only one day long?"

"The shows go on for a week, but I can't get away from the store for more than a couple of days. It just wears Mama out if she has to work in the store all day."

Dan Arthur nodded.

"Anyway, here's what I was going to tell you. I know you've been looking at big-screen TV's, and sometimes I can get some really good deals at the electronics show, so I was thinking that if I see one you might like, I could order it for you. It'll be a couple of months before it gets here, so you'll have time to save up, and if you don't want to buy it then, I can always sell it to somebody else."

After thinking for a moment, Dan Arthur said, "That would be great if you could find something for me at the show. I've been putting a few pennies back and I should be able to pay for it by the time it gets here."

Donnie smiled and said, "It'll be my pleasure to help you out."

Dan Arthur said, "I really appreciate that, especially after the hard time I gave you on the car thief thing."

Donnie said, "Oh, I meant to tell you. You know Teddy Jones that works over at cable TV? He told me that he's going to re-aim the surveillance cameras at Mike's Restaurant and the University Club so they won't be pointing at the sky anymore."

Dan Arthur replied, "That's great! Course we probably won't need to look at the tapes again for another five years."

Donnie laughed and said, "Maybe next time something happens it will be right in front of you so you catch it on your patrol car's dashboard camera."

"Dashboard camera." The words reverberated in Dan Arthur's head and he quickly stood up and said, "Donnie, I've got to go!"

Observing Dan Arthur's expression, Donnie asked, "Are you okay?"

As he headed toward the door, Dan Arthur replied, "I just remembered something I didn't remember remembering!"

CHAPTER 98

Dan Arthur almost ran across the street to the police station and headed immediately to the CSI room. Opening the storage cabinet marked "Dash Cam" he pulled out the recording from the night the stolen Mercedes had been abandoned in the University Club parking lot.

He attaching the portable disk drive to a computer and pressed the fast-forward key. Dan Arthur normally worked the three p.m. to eleven p.m. shift, but that night he had worked from eleven p.m. until seven a.m., and when the recording reached the eleven o'clock point he began scrutinizing it carefully.

Switching to slow motion when the recording showed Donnie's car on the street beside Cairn's house, Dan Arthur looked carefully at the periphery of the picture and could see the lights in the front of Cairn's house go off and a light at the rear of the house come on. Rewinding the recording, he looked at it again in slow motion and noted that no lights were on in Cairn's back yard.

He fast-forwarded, then switched to slow motion again when his patrol allowed him to see both Nicole's and Barbara's cars in their respective driveways.

Then he fast-forwarded until his patrol took him past Cairn's house for a second time, a little before two a.m. and that was when he saw what he didn't remember remembering.

When Cairn's house first came into view, he could clearly see that a light was on in the shed behind her house, but just before the house went out of view the light went off. He could also see that both Nicole's and Barbara's cars were now parked in front of Cairn's house.

Dan Arthur sat and mentally kicked himself for a moment. His keen observation abilities were a point of pride for him, but the recording showed he had missed quite a few things that particular night.

He had seen the light in the shed go off when he was patrolling but it had failed to register. True, at the time, there had been no real reason for him to note the event, but he was still concerned that he hadn't.

And while it was not unusual for the other Surfer Girls' cars to be in front of Cairn's house late at night, Dan Arthur felt he should have mentally noted it.

Pulling himself out of self-flagellation mode, Dan Arthur tried to discern some meaning for what he had seen.

There was a high-school kid named Bill something-or-another who worked at Mike's Restaurant, and when he got off work at midnight, he would usually drive around town listening to the radio for an hour or so before going home. It was a running joke among Delta City's policemen that around one o'clock in the morning they would drive by Bill's house and see if his car was in his driveway. If it was, they could find some place to pull over and take a nap because they knew that no one else would be out that late.

There was no reason why Cairn shouldn't go out to her shed in the middle of the night, neither was there any reason why Nicole and Barbara shouldn't come over to Cairn's house that late.

But Dan Arthur couldn't come up with any reason why those events might have happened on that particular night, and that bothered him.

CHAPTER 99

On Friday evening, Barbara pulled into Nicole's driveway shortly before 7:30 and parked behind Cairn's car.

Cairn was removing a large cardboard box from the trunk of her car, and when Barbara approached she said, "Did you bring the witch's tits, Barbara? I've got everything else."

Barbara grinned and said, "Cunt! Here, let me help you with that."

When Nicole opened the frond door it was all Cairn and Barbara could do to contain their laughter. Nicole was wearing a long black dress, and were it not for her blonde hair, 4-inch heels, and push-up bra she could have stepped straight out of Salem, Massachusetts, circa 1692.

All of the lights were off in the house, and Nicole carried a candle, telling Barbara and Cairn, "I thought we'd use the spare bedroom for our witching."

Several candles lit the spare bedroom, and Nicole had used what appeared to be black satin bed sheets to cover the windows and all of the furniture.

Nicole said, "Cairn, why don't you get all of your stuff set up while I get us some drinks."

When she left the room, Barbara said, "Knowing Nicole's housekeeping habits and the men she sleeps with I'm not sure I want to sit on these bed sheets. God knows what you might catch!"

Cairn laughed and said, "What is with that dress? She looks like that woman on TV with the big boobs that talks to dead people."

A minute later Nicole returned with a pitcher of margaritas and three glasses, Cairn opened one of the books of incantations, and the

Surfer Girls began casting the spells to kill the men who had done them wrong.

CHAPTER 100

Shortly after nine p.m., Dan Arthur's patrol took him by Nicole's house and he noticed that although the three Surfer Girl's cars were in the driveway, the house was dark except for a faint flickering behind the curtains in one window.

Deciding that was just one too many unusual things for the Surfer Girls, Dan Arthur accelerated his patrol car.

CHAPTER 101

Pulling his car to the side of the road beside Cairn's house, Dan Arthur turned on the emergency flashers and got out of his car in the same manner he normally would in a non-emergency situation.

He had radioed his location to the dispatcher, telling her he thought he had spotted a stray dog. While hardly cutting-edge police work, taking lost pets to the animal shelter was one of the duties of the Delta City Police Department, and it would make a good cover story if anyone should wonder what Dan Arthur was doing in Cairn's back yard.

Passing through an unlocked gate in the chain link fence, Dan Arthur walked toward Cairn's shed.

The shed door was also unlocked, so Dan Arthur pulled out his flashlight and began looking around the inside of the building.

It was almost empty, containing only a lawnmower that looked like it hadn't run in twenty years, a couple of one-gallon paint cans, and a large chest-style freezer. Dan Arthur noticed that spider webs covered everything in the shed, although the ones on the freezer had been disturbed, indicating that it had been opened recently.

Using his handkerchief to grasp the freezer's handle, he tried to open it and found it locked. Feeling around on a shelf above the freezer, he discovered a key, and opening the top, he shined his flashlight inside.

Then he just stood there.

In his many years of police work Dan Arthur had seen a number of dead bodies, in a lot of locations, and in a variety of conditions. However, none of his experience had prepared him to find the naked body of a dead man in a freezer that belonged to a woman he had known since high school.

Pointing his flashlight at the dead man's face, Dan Arthur recognized him from his mug shots as Terry Harding. Above one eye, he could see a long narrow bruise, but he didn't see any other injuries until he reached the man's penis, which bore what looked very much like a bite mark.

Some clothing was piled around the body's feet, and he checked the pockets for identification but found none.

Using the camera on his personal cell phone, Dan Arthur took pictures of the man's face, the bruise on his forehead, and the bite mark on his penis. Then, again using his handkerchief, Dan Arthur closed the lid on the freezer and replaced the key on the shelf.

Walking outside, Dan Arthur took a couple of pictures showing the freezer inside the building, and the shed's proximity to Cairn's house.

Back in his police car, Dan Arthur picked up the microphone, told the dispatcher that he had not been able to locate the stray dog, and asked if anyone had called it in.

Reasonably assured by the dispatcher's negative response that no one had noticed his visit to the shed, Dan Arthur resumed his patrol.

CHAPTER 102

Nicole had put the spell casting on hold while she left the room to mix another pitcher of margaritas.

In a low voice Barbara said, "Sometimes she makes me want to puke. I mean, even though it's just a goof, we are talking about killing people, and to Nicole it's just another Friday night party."

Measuring her words, Cairn asked, "What if it's not just a goof? What if these guys actually die because of our witchcraft?"

Barbara looked shocked as she said, "You don't actually think any of this is real, do you? C'mon, it's a goof, just like it was a goof when we were in high school."

"That's just it, Barbara. I'm not totally sure it was just a goof in high school, and I've seen a lot of strange stuff since then. Some weird shit happens during those Native American ceremonies out in New Mexico."

Whispering, "Cool it, Cairn. We can talk about it later," Barbara then raised her voice slightly she said, "And here comes Nicole with a bit of witch's brew for our parched throats!"

CHAPTER 103

After finding the dead man's body in Cairn's freezer, Dan Arthur had continued patrolling Delta City until the end of his shift. Then he went home and cracked open a brand new fifth of Jim Beam.

As he drank, Dan Arthur considered the differences between what he should do and what he was going to do, which could well be two very different things.

He was a police officer, sworn to uphold the law, but he knew that sometimes there were situations that the law just didn't cover, and he really wished that Bigfoot Newton were still around to give him some advice.

After inspiring him to become a cop, Bigfoot Newton had served as Dan Arthur's mentor during his first few years on the job. Even though Bigfoot had been nearing retirement, his cop instincts were still good, and he had taught Dan Arthur a lot about police work. But even more important, Bigfoot had taught Dan Arthur how to be a small-town cop.

Dan Arthur knew that it wouldn't take Bigfoot but a few seconds to come up with a plan for dealing with the body-in-Cairn's-freezer situation, but Bigfoot was now long in the grave and Dan Arthur would just have to figure out what to do on his own.

He didn't come up with a final solution that night, but he quickly found an interim one, and when the Jim Beam was gone, Dan Arthur went to bed.

CHAPTER 104

Sunday was his day off, and Dan Arthur was doing his weekly house cleaning when the phone rang.

"Dan Arthur, this is Harry Laird."

"What's up, Chief?"

"You know my brother over in Shreveport? His heart has started acting up on him again and they think he's gonna need some surgery."

"I'm sorry to hear that, Chief. I hope he's going to be okay."

"Well, it's kind of 'iffy' right now, Dan Arthur, so I'm going over there for a few days. Do you think you could drop by the department every couple of hours to check my messages and phone calls until I get back? I don't think there'll be much going on so you can probably handle things yourself, but if something big comes up you can call me."

"No problem at all, Chief. Go on over to Shreveport and take care of your brother. I'll give you a call if anything big comes up."

Hanging up the phone, Dan Arthur was happy that he would have some extra distractions over the next few days, as he had not yet decided what to do about the body in Cairn's freezer.

He knew he should report what he had seen in Cairn's shed, but he faced a problem. Since he hadn't really had what the lawyers call "probable cause" for poking around in the shed, what he had seen would not be admissible in court.

The lack of a search warrant wasn't an insurmountable problem, as it wouldn't take him more than a couple of minutes to figure out a story that would let him get one. But if he got a warrant, he would have to arrest Cairn, and he really didn't have anything to charge her with. The single bruise looked like the man fell and hit something, and with the bite mark on the man's penis, Dan Arthur's cop instincts told him it was probably some kind of self-defense thing.

An investigation might unearth more serious crimes, but right now the only thing Dan Arthur could charge Cairn with was something like concealing a body or interfering with an investigation.

Dan Arthur had verified the body was that of Terry Harding, and in his personal opinion Harding was now just another dead scumbag who didn't really merit any special effort toward finding his killer.

Harding's body had frozen solid, and while the Surfer Girls wouldn't have had too much trouble putting a limp body into the freezer, Dan Arthur knew getting a frozen one out would be quite a bit more difficult and he didn't think Harding would be going anywhere soon.

While Dan Arthur knew that anyone could make a mistake and take somebody's life, he just couldn't believe any of the Surfer Girls would deliberately kill someone, and he wanted to make sure whatever he did was the correct thing to do.

So, he decided that for the moment he would simply do nothing about the situation. The body would still be there when Chief Laird got back from Shreveport, and he would reconsider the situation then.

Picking up a basket of laundry, Dan Arthur resumed his house cleaning.

CHAPTER 105

Officer J.T. Gaines of the Monroe, Louisiana Police Department didn't really like writing speeding tickets before eight a.m., especially on a Monday, since most of the time it was just some poor citizen who had overslept and was trying to avoid being late for work.

But the driver of the car in front of him had not only been going 10 mph over the speed limit, he had also failed to come to a complete stop at a stop sign. So, even though it was still ten minutes until eight on a Monday, Officer Gaines knew he had better pull the car over. With a sigh, he reached down and flipped the switch that activated his blue light and pressed the button that would give a quick yelp of his siren.

When Officer Gaines reached the front door of the car, he saw the driver holding his license out the window and took it, saying, "Good morning sir."

Donnie Taylor said, "Officer, I am truly sorry for speeding. I overslept and I'm trying to get to the airport to catch a flight to Chicago."

Officer Gaines grinned and asked, "Are you sorry for blowing the stop sign also?"

Donnie sheepishly replied, "I didn't even know I did it, but I'm sorry about that, too."

Officer Gaines asked, "Is this your correct address in Delta City, Mr. Taylor?"

"Yes, sir."

"I'll tell you what, since you seem to be genuinely sorry about what you've done, I'll take your license back to my car and run a quick wants and warrants check, and if it comes back clean, I'll write you a warning ticket and you can be on your way."

As Officer Gaines wrote the warning ticket, his police radio came alive, saying, "Ten-seventeen".

Picking up the microphone he replied, "Ten-seventeen".

"Ten-seventeen, need a wellbeing check at 875 Virginia Street. Woman says she woke up and found her husband unresponsive."

Speaking into the microphone while getting out of his car, Officer Gaines replied, "Ten-seventeen's rolling on the call."

As he handed Donnie Taylor his license and the warning ticket, Officer Gaines said, "Take it slow when you're in Monroe, Mr. Taylor. There's always another airplane, but there's not another you."

Hurrying back to his patrol car, Officer Gaines turned on the siren and headed for 875 Virginia Street.

CHAPTER 106

Monday morning Dan Arthur tried to beat down his pile of paperwork while waiting for any phone calls that might come in for the absent Chief Laird.

After starting his regular patrol shift at three o'clock, Dan Arthur came back to the station at five p.m. to see if there were any additional messages for the chief.

There was one, from a Detective Bobby Joe McDonald with the Monroe Louisiana Police Department, but when Dan Arthur returned the call, the detective's voice mail advised him that Detective McDonald would be out of the office until ten o'clock Tuesday morning. Dan Arthur made a mental note to call him back then.

As he was leaving to resume his patrol, the dispatcher called out, "Dan Arthur! You know today's Nicole Bailey's birthday, don't you? I hear the other Surfer Girls are gonna be throwing a big party at Nicole's house."

"Shit!" Dan Arthur muttered under his breath, while aloud he said, "Well, I guess I'll be spending the night driving drunks home," and walked out to his patrol car.

CHAPTER 107

Making a hard left turn off Monroe Road a little after six p.m., Dan Arthur began driving north toward Nicole's house on South Main Street.

He saw Barbara's car approaching with its turn signal on, so he pulled his patrol car to the side of the road and walked behind Barbara's car up Nicole's driveway.

As she got out of her car, Barbara laughingly said, "Dan Arthur, you're way too early. The party doesn't start until eight!"

"Well, I'm afraid you'll have to start without me. I'm on patrol until eleven."

"Perfect, that's when things will really just be getting started. Why don't you come by when you finish your shift?" Looking very pointedly at Dan Arthur's crotch Barbara continued, "Nicole doesn't have a man in her life right now, maybe you could give her a special birthday present."

As his face slightly reddened Dan Arthur said, "No thanks, if I ever feel compelled to give Nicole a present I'll buy her something!"

Grinning, Barbara said, "Come on by anyway, you need a little fun in your life."

Dan Arthur smiled and said, "Oh I'm sure I'll have plenty of fun dealing with all of the drunks around here later. That's why I stopped. Do ya'll have any plans for keeping people from driving home drunk?"

"We sure do. We hired some high school boys, and if somebody is too drunk to drive, one of the boys will drive them home, and another kid will follow and bring the driver back here."

Dan Arthur laughed and said, "You always were the brains of the Surfer Girls, Barbara."

Barbara puffed out her chest and coquettishly said, "You mean you never admired me for my body?"

Dan Arthur ducked the question, saying, "You know I'm on duty, Barbara, and I like to keep my work and my personal life separate. Speaking of being on duty, I'd better get back to my patrol. I'll drive by here a couple of times tonight, and just call the station if you have any problems."

Settled into his patrol car, Dan Arthur happened to glance up the driveway where Barbara had bent over to get something out of the trunk of her car and he couldn't help but notice her attractive butt, complimented by her long, tan legs. Saying, *"Focus, Dan Arthur,"* he put the car in gear and pulled away.

Dan Arthur's mind began to drift as he slowly drove along. He thought, *"Give Nicole a special birthday present? Not damn likely!"* He had gone all the way through school with the Surfer Girls, and he had known by the second day of kindergarten that Nicole was nothing but a spoiled brat. Although he had been in a make-out session with Nicole once in middle school, she had seemed more interested in running her mouth than in kissing and being felt-up so his interest quickly waned.

Dan Arthur had always regarded Cairn as an enigma. By the time she was in high school she was beginning to do professional quality painting, and if Dan Arthur had ever bothered to own a painting it would have been the one with the dogs playing poker so they really didn't have much in common. He and Cairn had been lab partners in biology class and had become loose friends, but that was as far as it went.

Barbara was a different story. For as long as he could remember, Dan Arthur had considered her beautiful, and as the picture of Barbara bent over in Nicole's driveway replayed in his head he thought, *"Damned beautiful."*

Dan Arthur and Barbara had dated a few times during middle and high school. In the summer between their sophomore and junior years, Barbara had let Dan Arthur get to second base with her so she had frequently been in his head during his nightly jerk-off sessions.

Shortly after they started their junior year in high school, Barbara began her relationship with Bryan Selig and Dan Arthur started dating the girl he would later marry, which put an end to whatever romance they might have had.

After his divorce, Dan Arthur had considered asking Barbara out, but then he had thrown himself into his work and never called her.

They had been casual friends since then, although Barbara occasionally dropped a hint that she might be interested in at least a sexual relationship with him.

Lately, Dan Arthur had sometimes considered taking Barbara up on her hints. As he crossed the line into middle age he was no longer as interested in his work as he once was, and from time to time he was just plain lonely.

Driving his patrol car around the town square, Dan Arthur again thought about how sexy Barbara had looked in Nicole's driveway, and decided that he would at least think about asking her out the next time an opportunity presented itself.

CHAPTER 108

At the same time the Surfer Girls were finishing their preparations for Nicole's party in Delta City, Donnie Taylor was walking along Chicago's Wacker Drive, which runs parallel to the Chicago River through downtown.

Although stoves, refrigerators, and washers and dryers were the core of Delta City Appliance World's business, Donnie didn't find them anywhere near as fascinating as the latest TV's and home theater equipment. And since there were no groundbreaking new products on display at the appliance show, Donnie had quickly placed his orders and caught the shuttle bus back to downtown Chicago to catch his flight for Las Vegas.

His flight didn't leave until nine p.m., so Donnie planned to walk around downtown for a couple of hours, then go to the Thompson Center and catch a Blue Line EL train to O'Hare Airport.

Walking along Wacker Drive, Donnie did not know that the street was home to a number of advertising agencies, and that the building he was passing housed the agency where Cairn had worked during her disastrous year in Chicago.

A blaring car horn caught Donnie's attention and he looked up just in time to see a CTA bus hit a car that had swerved in front of it. The force of the impact drove the car into a light pole less than five feet from where he was standing.

Under a minute later, a police car pulled up and an officer jumped out and began checking on the driver of the car. Shortly after, a siren announced the arrival of a fire truck, and the paramedics from the truck took over care of the injured motorist.

Walking toward the knot of people who had gathered around the accident scene, the policeman asked in a loud voice, "Did anybody see what happened?"

Donnie spoke up, saying, "I did, sir."

The policeman quickly wrote down Donnie's version of the accident, along with his name and address, then moved on to another witness.

As Donnie walked away from the scene, a man in a suit approached the policeman, pointed to the wrecked car, and asked, "Did the guy make it?"

The policeman replied, "Hello, Detective Scala. He looks a little beat up but I think he'll be okay. What brings you down here?"

Detective Scala pointed to the building that housed Cairn's old advertising agency and replied, "Looks like they found a dead body up there." With a grin he continued, "Why don't you come up to the 40th floor after you finish here and see how the real cops do it?"

The policeman said, "Real cops my ass. But I'll come up there and give you guys a few lessons after I'm done."

CHAPTER 109

Shortly before ten p.m., Dan Arthur Truman was making his second pass of the evening by Nicole Bailey's house. While his first drive by had revealed a moderately rowdy party just getting started, he could now see that Nicole's birthday celebration was well on its way to becoming a legendary Surfer Girls drunk fest.

Barbara was putting an obviously inebriated couple into a car driven by one of the high school boys, and seeing Dan Arthur she waved for him to stop.

Walking over to the police car, Barbara said, "See, Dan Arthur, we've got the driver thing going just like I told you we would, so you can go find you a place to take a nap. Everybody in town is either here or safely home in bed."

Dan Arthur mock-growled, "Smart ass," then asked, "How's the party going?"

"Great, Dan Arthur, just like all of the Surfer Girls' parties. Cairn and I are counting down until Nicole hauls her boobs out, which she'll probably do in about five minutes. Want to come in and have a look?"

With a groan, Dan Arthur said, "God no! If I saw Nicole's boobs I'd probably never want to have sex again!"

Barbara pulled her tee shirt up about an inch above her navel and said, "So what would happen if I showed you my boobs, Dan Arthur?"

The policeman smiled and said, "Since you're out here on a public street, I'd have to arrest you!"

After yanking her shirt up to just below her bra, Barbara quickly lowered it and said, "See you later, Dan Arthur. I better get back to the party."

Driving away, Dan Arthur thought, "*Maybe I will give her a call.*"

CHAPTER 110

Tuesday morning at ten o'clock, Dan Arthur picked up the phone in Chief Laird's office and dialed the number of Bobby Joe McDonald, the detective who had called from Monroe, Louisiana the previous day.

"Detective bureau, McDonald speaking."

"Detective McDonald, this is Dan Arthur Truman from the Delta City Arkansas Police Department. You called Chief Laird yesterday. The chief's out dealing with a family emergency so I'm handling his calls. I tried to reach you yesterday but got your voice mail. What can I help you with?"

Detective McDonald replied, "Actually it's good that you didn't catch me yesterday. I just got a medical examiner's report about a half hour ago that makes the case I'm calling you about even weirder."

Dan Arthur said, "Okay, I got my pen and paper, so why don't you tell me what you got."

"We took a 911 call early Monday morning from a woman who said she'd just gotten out of bed and found her husband unresponsive with his head down on the kitchen table."

Dan Arthur said, "Okay."

"The responding officer couldn't rouse him either and called for the paramedics, who said he was dead. The paramedics did a quick examination of the body and they couldn't find any indications as to cause of death. The wife told us he was 46 years old and in good health. Name was 'David Henson'."

Writing quickly, Dan Arthur said, "Un-huh, got it."

"The reason I called you yesterday was because when the responding officer lifted the man's head, he found an old cocktail napkin underneath him. It was from a place called the 'Louisville

Lounge' that used to be a popular spot with the kids back in the 80's. It shut down about 15 years ago. Anyway, 'Barbara Mason' and a phone number was written in a woman's handwriting on the back of the napkin, and underneath, the word 'cunt' was written three times, in what the vic's wife said was Henson's handwriting. All of the writing was pretty faded, so it was probably written some time back."

Dan Arthur said, "We've got a Barbara Mason here in Delta City. Early 40's. All of the kids from up here used to go to Monroe a lot back in the 80's. Was it a Delta City phone number?"

Detective McDonald said, "Yes, that's the reason I called your chief. I checked with the telephone company and they told me that the phone number had been reassigned several times since the 80's."

Dan Arthur asked, "Do you want me to talk to Barbara and see if she knows this David Henson?"

"I'd appreciate that, if it's not too much trouble, but there's a little more to this thing."

Dan Arthur asked, "What's that?"

"You remember I said I had just got the medical examiner's report? Seems the ME can't find any reason why this guy died. Course we'll have to wait for the final tox results, but the preliminary screens don't show any kind of drugs at all in Henson's system. The folks down at the ME's office are really scratching their heads over this one. It looks like this guy just sat down at the table and died."

Dan Arthur said, "That is kinda strange."

"And like that TV fella says, 'But wait, that's not all!' Turns out that right before my officer responded to the Henson call he had just written a warning ticket about four blocks away for a fella from Delta City. You know anything about a Donald Taylor?"

Dan Arthur couldn't contain his laughter as he said, "Barbara Mason is one of three women here in Delta City that we call the Surfer Girls. Donnie Taylor's been mooning after them since high school, but they don't even know he exists. It's a joke around here that if a Surfer Girl is around Donnie Taylor ain't far away."

Detective McDonald said, "A fella with a tinfoil hat could make all kind of stuff out of that. Somewhere along the way, Barbara Mason gave her phone number to a guy who died for no reason and around the time we find the dead guy we come across Donnie Taylor, who sometimes follows Barbara Mason around, a few blocks away from where the dead guy lived. Recon there's anything to be made out of it?"

Dan Arthur laughed again and said, "My personal opinion is that it's just one hell of a coincidence. I spoke with Donnie a couple of days ago. He owns a TV and appliance store here in town, and he told me he would be going down to Monroe to catch a plane. He was going to Chicago so he could look at the new model stoves and refrigerators. You did say the writing on the napkin looked old, so it's probably one of those random things that happen sometimes."

Detective McDonald said, "Since you know the folks involved I'll go by your judgment, but I'd appreciate it if you'd run this thing down with Barbara Mason and Donald Taylor and let me know whatever you find out. And I'll give you a ring when I get the tox results back on this Henson fella."

Dan Arthur said, "Barbara usually has lunch at a place right across from the station, so I'll run over there in a bit and see if I can catch up to her. Donnie said he would be going to Las Vegas for an electronics show after he finishes up in Chicago, but I'll talk to him when he gets back."

"Thank you very much, Officer Truman, and I'll look forward to talking to you again soon."

After he hung up the phone, Dan Arthur just sat there for a moment. He had more or less blown the whole thing off when he was talking to Detective McDonald, but he did find the events a bit off-putting, especially since he also knew about the body in Cairn's freezer.

Dan Arthur thought, *"There is definitely some strange things going on!"*

The intercom on the chief's desk buzzed and the dispatcher said, "Detective Scala from Chicago called while you were on the phone."

"Did he say what he wanted?"

"No, he just asked for Chief Laird. I told him the chief was out and that you were covering for him, but you were on the phone. He was real nice for somebody from Chicago and asked if you could call him back around two o'clock this afternoon."

Dan Arthur said, "I'll give him a call," and returned his paperwork mountain.

CHAPTER 111

As Dan Arthur was talking to Detective McDonald on the phone Donnie Taylor was getting ready to check out of his hotel room in Las Vegas, where it was shortly after eight o'clock in the morning.

He had picked up his bag and was heading toward the door when the phone rang and Donnie hesitated as he considered whether to answer it. The only person who knew where he was staying was his mother, who had his cell phone number, and if it was somebody from the hotel staff, he could find out what it was when he got to the front desk.

But the phone continued to ring so Donnie said, "Oh, hell," and answered it.

"Mr. Taylor, this is James Hernandez. I'm the security director of the hotel."

Donnie replied, "Yes sir. Is there a problem?"

James Hernandez said, "I'm sorry to trouble you, be we have a security situation and we need to evacuate you from your room for a few minutes. In just a moment, one of my security men will knock on your door very softly and hold his ID in front of the peephole in the door. Please come out of your room and follow his instructions."

"I was just preparing to check out. Would it be okay if I just brought my suitcase with me?"

"That will be fine."

At that moment, Donnie heard a tapping on the door and after checking the security man's ID through the peephole, he opened it.

A well-dressed man roughly the size of a Mack truck quietly said, "Mr. Taylor, this way please," and led Donnie down the hallway to the elevator lobby.

Donnie was amazed at the collection of people in the elevator lobby. Several appeared to be hotel guests, others appeared to be hotel security from their size and dress, and there was a police SWAT team wearing bulletproof vests and carrying automatic weapons.

One of the man-mountains stepped up to Donnie, extended his hand, and said, "Mr. Taylor, I'm James Hernandez, the hotel security director." Pointing toward the opposite side of the elevator lobby he continued, "Let's go over here where we can talk for a minute or two and you can be on your way."

When they were out of earshot of the group, Hernandez said, "Mr. Taylor, we have a security issue. We believe that the man who occupied the room next to yours may be a person the police are interested in." He held up a computer printout and asked, "Just in case we need to get in touch with you, is this your correct name and contact information?"

Donnie looked at the paper and said, "Yes, that's all correct."

Hernandez said, "Thank you. I know that you didn't check in until late in the evening, but did you hear any kind of unusual noises or anything like that coming from the room next door?"

"No, I was pretty tired after my flight so I went to bed right after I checked in. And I'm a pretty heavy sleeper so even if there was some noise I might not have heard it."

The security director scrawled something on the back of a business card and handed it to Donnie, saying, "Mr. Taylor, thank you very much for your cooperation. Someone from the Las Vegas Police Department will probably be contacting you in the next couple of days. Give this card to the member of the hotel management staff who will greet you when you get off the elevator and your stay here will be compliments of the hotel. And please don't mention this to anyone else as we're not extending this courtesy to the other guests."

Donnie smiled and said, "Thank you, Mister Hernandez. I knew I should have ordered steak and lobster from room service last night."

With a tight smile, the security officer led Donnie back to the bank of elevators. As the elevator door closed, Donnie could see James Hernandez talking intently with the members of the SWAT team.

About the time Donnie's elevator reached the hotel lobby, James Hernandez slid his keycard into the slot, eased open the door of the room adjacent to Donnie's, and stepped back as the SWAT team rushed in.

Hernandez entered when the SWAT team leader called "Clear!" He saw a man sitting in a chair with his head slumped down and walked over to check for a pulse.

The man, later identified as "Andrew James", "Buford Donaldson", and several other aliases, was dead.

James Hernandez picked up some papers that were lying on the dead man's lap and looked at them.

They were a divorce decree, ending the marriage of Andrew James and Nicole Bailey.

CHAPTER 112

Dan Arthur entered Café on the Square about ten minutes after noon, and seeing the Surfer Girls were at their usual table, he walked over.

Cairn saw him first and said, "Hi, Dan Arthur!"

"Hello ladies. Barbara, can I talk to you for a second?"

"Sure thing, Dan Arthur. Sit down and join us."

With a grin Dan Arthur said, "I'd love to, but this is for Barbara's ears only."

Nicole and Cairn exchanged glances as Barbara stood up and followed Dan Arthur out the front door, then began whispering excitedly.

Outside the café, Dan Arthur said, "Barbara, I've got something I need to discuss with you. Can you come over to the station around 2:30?"

Barbara replied, "I'm going to Pine Bluff for a seminar on advanced rehabilitation techniques when I finish lunch, but I'll be back around ten tonight if you want to stop by my house."

"Barbara, I'm afraid it's official business, and I'll be on patrol until eleven."

"If it's really important, just come by the house after you finish your shift, Dan Arthur. And I'll keep it strictly business."

"Okay, I'll be there around eleven fifteen."

When Barbara returned to the Surfer Girl's table Nicole immediately said, "Don't worry, Barbara, I'll loan you bail money!"

Looking concerned, Cairn asked, "What did he want, Barbara?"

"Oh, he just told me he wanted to come over and stick his big old cop dick in me. I told him I'd get a banana and practice my blow jobs until he got there."

Nicole barely managed to avoid spitting out a mouthful of coffee as she laughed and said, "Don't forget to bring us some pictures!"

Popping the last of her sandwich into her mouth, Barbara said, "I'll make videos! I'm off to Pine Bluff, see you guys tomorrow."

CHAPTER 113

Leaving Café on the Square, Dan Arthur found himself drawn to the drugstore a half block up the street, where he picked up a bottle of Polo cologne. He tried to convince himself that it was only because he would be a little bit sweaty and stinky after he finished his patrol shift, but deep down he knew he wouldn't have bought it if he were going to talk to a male after work.

Back in Chief Laird's office shortly after two p.m., Dan Arthur dialed the number of the Chicago Police Department and asked for Detective Scala.

A few seconds later, someone came on the phone and said, "Scala."

"Detective Scala, this is Officer Dan Arthur Truman from Delta City, Arkansas. I understand you called me earlier."

The detective said, "Yeah, hang on a second." Dan Arthur could hear what sounded like papers being shuffled, then Detective Scala said, "Here it is. Okay, I've got a death investigation and the names of a couple of your citizens popped up."

"So, what have you got?"

Detective Scala said, "Vic's name was Jared DeCosta. He was some kind of a heavy hitter with one of the big advertising agencies here. Body was found by one Linda Devinie, who worked under him, and I mean that in the literal sense."

As Dan Arthur laughed the detective continued, "When we found the body there wasn't a mark on him or any other indication of how he died. He was just sitting in a big chair at his desk."

Dan Arthur said, "That seems to be going around. I got a call about a similar death in Monroe, Louisiana earlier today."

Detective Scala laughed and said, "Where's Mulder and Scully when we need them? Anyway, I used to do undercover narcotics back in the mid 80's, and this Linda Devinie used to spend a lot of time powdering her nose in some of the bars here, if you get my drift. I never heard too much about DeCosta, but he was frequently in the right place at a lot of the right times and quite a few advertising people were total cokeheads back in the day."

Dan Arthur said, "That whole cocaine thing pretty much skipped us. We just went straight from pot to meth about ten years ago."

Detective Scala said, "Yeah, we got that too. Anyway, given all of the history, I figured that maybe DeCosta just took one too many toots and bought the big one. But we didn't find any drugs in his office, and when the paramedics got here they said it didn't look like he died from an overdose. It'll be sometime tomorrow before I get the autopsy report, but right now this looks like it's going to be a strange one."

Dan Arthur laughed and said, "I guess that's why they pay us the big bucks!"

The detective said, "Yeah, right. Tell that to my wife. Anyway, when we found the body there was an employment application from 1986 on his desk. The applicant's name was, hang on, Karen Lynn Dumont, nickname spelled 'C-A-I-R-N', with an address on Main Street in Delta City, Arkansas. Linda Devinie told me that Dumont had worked at the advertising agency for about a year in 86 or so, then just up and quit. I leaned on Ms. Devinie a bit and she told me that Dumont had hooked up with Jared DeCosta to do a little partying one night, and he had apparently indicated he might give her a promotion in exchange for services rendered. Then the next day he announced that he would be moving to New York to run the agency's office there, and according to Linda Devinie, Ms. Dumont was more than a little unhappy about it."

Dan Arthur let out a low whistle and said, "Our Cairn has been keeping secrets. By the way, she started spelling her name 'C-A-I-R-N' cause that's the way all of us rednecks pronounced it."

Detective Scala laughed and said, "Go with the flow, huh. So what can you tell me about Ms. Dumont?"

"I've known her since we were kids. She's an artist, always been kinda quiet. I heard something about her living in Chicago, but when she moved back here she had been living in Taos, New Mexico for eighteen years or so. She's a pretty well-known artist and she makes a good living selling her pictures."

The detective said, "Sounds like Chicago was just a walk on the wild side for her, and it looks like she got out just in time."

Dan Arthur asked, "Is there anything you want me to have a little chat with Cairn about?"

"Let's hold off on Ms. Dumont until I hear from the medical examiner on DeCosta's cause of death. But there's another Delta City citizen mixed up in all of this." There was again a sound of shuffling papers, and Detective Scala continued, "Shortly after DeCosta's body was found a CTA bus smacked into a car right outside the advertising agency building, and one of the witnesses was a Donald Taylor who gave a Delta City address."

Dan Arthur tried to keep his voice steady as he said, "I know Donnie, he runs a TV and appliance store. He told me he was going to Chicago for a day for some sort of appliance show, and after that he was going to fly to Las Vegas for an electronics show."

Detective Scala said, "Mr. Taylor could have walked a block from where all this happened and caught an EL train to the airport, so his being there was probably just a coincidence. Tell you what, let me get back to you after I get a cause of death on DeCosta and if I need anything from Dumont or Taylor I'll let you know. No sense bothering the citizens unnecessarily."

"Sounds good to me. Call me after you hear from the ME and I'll give you whatever help you need."

Hanging up the phone, Dan Arthur thought, "*I'm glad you don't want to upset my citizens, but you've sure as hell upset me!*"

And after a few seconds consideration, he decided that he wouldn't put on any of the Polo cologne before going out to Barbara's house.

CHAPTER 114

Driving back from Pine Bluff, Barbara really tried to keep her mind on the information she'd picked up at the physical therapy seminar, but her thoughts kept drifting back toward her upcoming meeting with Dan Arthur.

Her thoughts ran in two different directions. While she had decided that she really wanted to fuck Dan Arthur, and hoped to do it that night, she was mildly concerned about the "official business" thing.

Between the events surrounding the death of Terry Harding and Nicole's witchcraft fixation, Barbara had simply not been able to muster up the time or energy to drive the five or so miles to where the nearest man she regularly slept with lived. Besides, she was frankly becoming bored with most of the men she had been screwing.

Barbara laughed as she once again thought, *"Too bad Cairn and I aren't lesbians!"*

Along the way, both Barbara and Cairn had been in a couple of three-ways with another woman and a man, and both had agreed that while sex with a woman had been interesting, they really preferred men.

Despite that, one night Barbara and Cairn had gotten really drunk and tried to have sex, but they had both been overcome with laughter before anything actually happened. After that, they decided that while they would share everything else in their lives, they would enjoy their sex separate and apart.

Barbara sometimes wondered why she and Dan Arthur had not gotten together, and she always felt like if the planets had ever properly aligned it would have happened.

She had always liked Dan Arthur, and when they were in high school, she found him quite sexy. He played football and baseball and was nicely muscled, and he bulked-up a bit while he was in the service. Since there was only one gym in Delta City, Barbara often saw Dan Arthur shirtless there and knew that he still stayed in good shape.

However, when Dan Arthur returned from the Army and joined the Delta City Police Department, Barbara pretty much decided that, to quote an old song, Jupiter would never align with Mars for the two of them.

She tried not to be elitist, but Barbara liked to live well and knew that she wouldn't be able to do it on a small-town cop's salary, so she allowed Dan Arthur to drop off her radar.

But things had changed over the years. Barbara now had a very good income from the hospital, the house she had built would soon be paid for, and her parents had left her well provided for in their wills. If she and Dan Arthur were to get together now they would both be able to live well, assuming that his masculine ego didn't get in the way.

Pulling into her driveway, Barbara decided official business be damned, she was definitely going to make a strong play for Dan Arthur and see how it worked out.

In her bedroom, she took off the professional-looking pantsuit she had worn to the physical therapy seminar and began trying to decide what to wear for her attack on Dan Arthur.

She put on a red see-through bra, added a thin white tee shirt, and completed the ensemble with a thong and cut-off jeans. She nodded in satisfaction as a glance in the mirror revealed the slight bumps of her nipples through her shirt.

A quick look at the state of her pedicure assured her that her bare feet would be okay, so she spritzed on a little of her favorite cologne and went into her living room.

Barbara was inherently a neat person, so it only took her a couple of seconds to put the living room into perfect shape. Just as she finished adjusting the lights to provide the proper seductive atmosphere, she heard a car pulling up in front of her house. Impulsively, she opened the refrigerator door and stuck her breasts into the cool cabinet.

Stepping back, she saw that her nipples were sticking out very nicely and thought, *"There's no way he'll miss those babies,"* as she went to answer Dan Arthur's knock on her door.

CHAPTER 115

Dan Arthur immediately noticed Barbara's erect nipples and said, "Barbara, would you mind putting on an over-shirt and turning the lights up a bit? I really do need to have a serious discussion with you."

Barbara smiled and replied "Dan Arthur, you're no fun at all!" She flipped the lights on in the kitchen, and said, "Why don't we sit in there? I'll be right back."

Returning from the bedroom buttoning up a blue and white striped man's dress shirt, Barbara said, "I guess you probably aren't interested in a drink and I don't have any coffee made, so would some bottled water or a Coke be okay?"

"A Coke would be fine."

Placing a glass on the table in front of Dan Arthur, Barbara said, "Okay, I'm in 'strictly business' mode, so what's up?"

Glancing at his notebook, Dan Arthur asked, "Barbara, do you know a man from Monroe named David Henson?"

Barbara flinched and took on an expression of wariness as she replied, "Man is far too good a term for that son-of-a-bitch. Let's say I once knew a worm from Monroe named David Henson. Why?"

"He was found dead a couple of days ago. How well did you know him?"

In a cold voice, Barbara replied, "I picked him up in a bar in Monroe one night when I was in college and we went to his apartment. He couldn't get it up, I started bitching at him, and he hit me a couple of times and raped me."

In a sympathetic voice Dan Arthur said, "I never heard anything about it. Did you report it to the Monroe police?"

"C'mon Dan Arthur. No offense, but it was in Monroe, Louisiana in 1984. I went home with the guy, got naked, and got in bed with him. Just how far do you think I'd have gotten with a rape claim?"

"Yeah, I know. Did you have any marks or anything?"

"I had a bruise and a cut lip and I took some pictures of them. Later I showed Cairn the pictures and we talked about the whole thing for a while, then after that, I put it behind me and moved on with my life. Why are you asking me about that shit now?"

Dan Arthur said, "When the Monroe police found Henson dead, underneath the body there was a napkin from the Louisville Lounge with your name and your parent's phone number on it."

Barbara said, "That's where I picked him up, and I probably did give him my number there in the bar. So, how did he die?"

"That's the problem, Barbara. Monroe tells me their medical examiner hasn't been able to find a cause of death. It looks like Henson just died for no reason."

Remembering the incantations she had chanted, Barbara thought, "*Oh, shit! But it couldn't have been our witchcraft that killed him, that was just a goof!*"

Dan Arthur saw a brief expression of shock cross Barbara's face, but given the circumstances, he couldn't really read anything from it. Continuing his questioning, he asked, "You know Donnie Taylor, don't you?"

"Who?"

"Donnie Taylor, he went to high school with us and owns Delta City Appliance World."

Barbara said, "I don't remember him. The only times I've been in the appliance store an older woman waited on me."

Thinking, "*Poor Donnie,*" Dan Arthur said, "Funny thing, Donnie's always had a major thing for the Surfer Girls, and I don't think he's ever been more than five feet from one of you since he moved to Delta City. You never noticed him around?"

With a puzzled look Barbara said, "No, I don't think I've ever seen him. Has he been, like, stalking us?"

Dan Arthur said, "He isn't like a true stalker, I think he just wanted one of the Surfer Girls to notice him and I guess none of you ever did."

"I don't know this Donnie Taylor and I never saw him stalking us, so why are you asking me about him?"

"Is there any way Donnie Taylor could have known about David Henson raping you?"

"Not from me. The only person I ever told about it was Cairn, and I don't think she would have told anyone since we both know how to keep secrets. You know, Dan Arthur, you're kinda freaking me out with all of this."

Dan Arthur said, "I'm sorry, I don't think there's anything to any of this, but I do have one more question. I saw you around town several times in the last few days so just for the record, where were you Sunday and Monday?"

Barbara replied, "Like you said, I was right here in Delta City."

Closing his notebook, Dan Arthur said, "That's it. I may need to ask you a few questions later, but we're done for now."

Barbara flashed a quick smile and said, "So it's like on TV, I'm free to go? Not under arrest or anything?"

Dan Arthur returned the smile and said, "You're free to go, but since it's your house, I'd better get going."

Barbara looked at the policeman and said, "No, that's not the way it works, Dan Arthur. You took up my time with your official business, and now I expect you to have a drink with me and fuck me."

Dan Arthur was not particularly surprised by this turn of events. He had believed for a while that it was just a matter of time in coming, and had spent some time thinking about how he would handle an invitation like this from Barbara.

As far as the police department was concerned, as long as the person a police officer was involved with was not a habitual criminal and there was no favoritism by the officer, there would be no problem. But Dan Arthur considered himself to be a professional law enforcement officer, and he felt that while the department's rules and regulations set a minimum standard for conduct, in many cases he should set his personal minimums somewhat higher.

But right now, even with all of his thought and preparation, Dan Arthur wasn't sure how he should respond to Barbara.

Before the phone call from Monroe, he would have gone for it without hesitation. Barbara hadn't even gotten a traffic ticket in the last ten years, and he had once heard her say something about having to quit smoking pot when the hospital where she worked instituted random drug testing. He was quite certain that Barbara had not been involved in anything illegal for years.

But now she was involved in the unexplained death of David Henson, even if only peripherally, and there was also the matter of the dead body in Cairn's freezer, which Dan Arthur believed Barbara was probably somehow connected with.

He really wanted to go to bed with Barbara, whether for a one-night stand or as the beginning of a longer-term relationship, and he was painfully aware that were he to stand up right now it would look like he had shoved his nightstick down the front of his pants. So, he turned to the higher power who had often given him guidance in questions of cop morality, and asked himself, "What would Bigfoot do?"

Dan Arthur remembered a discussion he once had with Bigfoot where they were discussing what made a good small town cop. Bigfoot had said, "If you aren't willing to arrest your best friend you can't be a good small town cop. If you aren't willing to arrest your mother or you father or your brother or your wife you can't be a good small town cop. It ain't like the big city where you can get another officer to handle stuff like that. You're the cop, so you have to do it. That doesn't mean you can't be friends with people and you can't love people, but you have to accept that a day may come when you have to lock up someone you really care for. And if you can't do that, you need to move on to a big city police department, because you won't be able to be a good small town cop."

With Bigfoot's admonition firmly lodged in his brain, Dan Arthur looked at Barbara, who was giving him an expectant stare, and asked, "Do you have any Jack Daniels?"

CHAPTER 116

The following morning Dan Arthur woke up next to Barbara, and managed to get out of bed and get dressed without waking her. Then he just stood there for a minute trying to figure out what to do next.

He wasn't quite sure if last night had just been a one-night stand or if it was the beginning of something more. So he didn't want to seem pushy, but he didn't want to just walk out cold either.

After a few moments of thought, he took a page out of his notebook, wrote "Dan Arthur's personal cell phone" and his phone number, and propped the note up on the nightstand.

When he walked out her front door, Dan Arthur suddenly realized that his pickup truck had been parked in front of Barbara's house all night. Fortunately, she lived on a cul-de-sac with very little traffic, so the likelihood of anyone even seeing his truck was small, and the likelihood of them knowing it was his truck was even smaller.

But there was one person he really hoped hadn't seen his truck there, and he could only pray that the officer on the overnight shift had not found it necessary to come by Barbara's house while on patrol.

CHAPTER 117

A little after ten a.m. Dan Arthur entered the police station to check Chief Laird's messages. Even though it was the Fourth of July holiday, he knew that fighting crime was a 24/7/365 endeavor so he settled into the chief's chair and went to work.

The first message was from Chief Laird, and said that his brother was worse so he wouldn't be back into the office until the following Monday. Dan Arthur made a mental note to call the chief later in the day just to touch base.

As he looked at the next message, Dan Arthur couldn't help exclaiming, "What the fuck?"

The Delta City Police Department frequently received messages from police departments in adjacent counties, and maybe once a week they would get one from another department in Arkansas or a surrounding state, but it was only every couple of months that they received a message from a police department outside of the region.

Now they had received three in as many days.

The message was from Detective Vince Rayburn of the Las Vegas Police Department, and with no idea how prescient he was, Dan Arthur laughed as he thought, *"Monroe was about Barbara and Chicago was about Cairn, so Las Vegas must be about Nicole."*

Glancing at the clock and seeing it was 10:15, Dan Arthur thought, *"That's 8:15 in Las Vegas, so I'll give Detective Rayburn a chance to have a cup of coffee before I call him back."*

The next two messages were from Detective McDonald in Monroe and Detective Scala in Chicago, and both indicated that they had medical examiner's reports they wanted to discuss with him.

Picking up the phone, Dan Arthur dialed Detective McDonald's number.

"Detective McDonald."

"Detective McDonald, this is Officer Truman with the Delta City Police Department. I understand you got the ME's report back on that David Henson who died the other day."

"Thanks for calling me back, Officer Truman. I'm afraid we got one hell of a mystery on our hands."

Dan Arthur laughed and replied, "It's a holiday, what did you expect?"

Detective McDonald also laughed and said, "Ain't it the truth! Anyway, our ME couldn't come up with a cause of death for Henson so he overnighted some samples to the state police crime lab in Baton Rouge. So while it's evident that he is dead, neither medical examiner can tell us why he's dead. There's no trauma, his heart and brain and other organs are perfect, and there were no drugs or other toxic substances in his system. So what we have is a man who sat down at the kitchen table and died for no reason whatsoever."

Dan Arthur tried to sound sympathetic as he said, "Better you than me, Detective McDonald. By the way, I talked to Barbara Mason, the woman whose name was on the bar napkin. She told me she had gotten with David Henson one night at the Louisville Lounge when she was back in college. She told me they went to Henson's apartment but he was a little limp in the linguini, if you know what I mean, and she went off on him."

As Detective McDonald laughed Dan Arthur said, "And believe me, if Barbara went off on him he would have been feeling even smaller than his dick was. Anyway, Henson apparently lost it and hit Barbara a couple of times, then raped her."

Detective McDonald asked, "Did she file a police report?"

Dan Arthur replied, "No. It was back in 1984 and since she had willingly gone home with the guy she didn't think your department would do anything about it. She didn't want to deal with the BS associated with filing a complaint, so she just put it out of her head and moved on."

Detective McDonald said, "I'm sorry she didn't file a report, it would have saved us some trouble over the years. But I know what you mean about how things were back then. We have a couple of older cops here who still act like assholes, but we're trying to weed them out."

Dan Arthur said, "I wasn't on the job back then, but I imagine if it wasn't a local person the same sort of thing would have happened up here. It was a different time back then, and thank God it's mostly gone."

"Amen," said Detective McDonald.

"I believe you said something about it would have saved you some trouble if Barbara had filed a report?"

Detective McDonald said, "I guess it was about a year after the incident with Barbara Mason citizen that Henson got married and for the next year we were out at his house about once a week on a domestic violence complaint. But his wife would never sign a complaint and back then there wasn't much we could do without her filing charges. Finally though she'd had enough and she left him."

Dan Arthur said, "If he'd been locked up it would have kept him out of your hair, but that's the way it goes sometimes."

Detective McDonald said, "No kidding. But I guess his wife leaving him made him see the light. One of my officers told me Henson spent some time in an anger management program and it seems to have worked. He got remarried a couple of years ago and we hadn't been out to his house until his wife found him dead."

Dan Arthur said, "By the way, Barbara was here in town for the last few days, so I don't think she was involved in his death. Is there any chance one of Henson's wives did him in?"

"No, we talked to both of them and I don't think they're involved either. His first wife moved to Dallas and remarried, and when I talked to her it didn't sound like she was carrying a grudge. And since Henson didn't have much life insurance his current wife is going to have a tough time making ends meet, so that pretty much rules her out. And we couldn't find any motive for anybody else to kill him."

Dan Arthur said, "I sure don't envy you on this one."

Detective McDonald asked, "Did you have a chance to talk to that Donald Taylor who got pulled over a few blocks from Henson's house right before we found the body?"

"No, I don't think he got back to Delta City until last night and I was on patrol from three until eleven. I'll see if I can track him down in a couple of hours if you want me to, but we've got a Fourth of July barbeque on the town square and I wanted to go over there for a little while before I start my patrol shift."

Detective McDonald laughed and said, "Officer Truman, I'm making a special request that you not talk to Taylor today. That way you can go to your barbeque and I can go home and spend the afternoon with my family. Right now I don't think there's anything that can't keep 'til tomorrow, so as far as I'm concerned things can wait until then."

Dan Arthur said, "I'm with you on that! I'll call you tomorrow after I talk to Donnie Taylor."

After he hung up the phone, Dan Arthur walked outside to watch the activity. It was a tradition for all of the restaurants in town to close on the Fourth of July, set up a stand, and sell their food on the square.

After seeing that the crew from Mike's Restaurant was out in full force, Dan Arthur walked back to the police locker room. Mike's was known throughout the area for having the best barbeque around, and Dan Arthur knew that despite his best efforts he would end up overeating. He opened the door to his locker, and after making sure that his "loose" uniform was clean, walked back to Chief Laird's office to call Detective Scala in Chicago.

CHAPTER 118

The voice on the telephone said, "Scala," and Dan Arthur replied, "Detective Scala? This is Officer Truman from the Delta City Police Department. I got a message that you had received the medical examiner's report on Jared DeCosta."

Dan Arthur could hear the sound of papers being shuffled as Detective Scala said, "DeCosta, DeCosta, got it! You enjoying your holiday, Officer Truman?"

"About as much as you are. Sounds like you've got a lot of cases to handle."

Detective Scala replied, "Too damn many, and my precinct is one of the quieter ones. Okay, it looks like Mr. DeCosta died of, what the fuck? The ME's report says 'no definitive cause of death could be determined'. Hang on, let me scan this quickly." A couple of seconds later Detective Scala said, "Officer Truman, the ME's telling us that even with all of their tests they couldn't find out why DeCosta died."

Dan Arthur said, "I just got the same thing from Monroe, Louisiana on a death they have there. Neither the local ME or their state police ME could find any reason why the guy died, and I've got the feeling I'm going to find the same situation with another death I'll be looking into a little later today."

Detective Scala asked, "You got a guess as to what happened to these guys?"

"Right now the only thing that comes to mind is some hard-to-trace poison."

Detective Scala said, "That's about the only thing I can come up with, too. Now, I believe you offered to interview one of your citizens, a Cairn Dumont, when we talked the other day. Would you mind having a chat with her? Not today though, I'm getting the fuck out of here the minute I hang up the phone!"

Dan Arthur laughed and said, "No problem, I'll have a talk with Cairn tomorrow. I've got one more phone call to make and then I'll also be out of here. We always have a little Fourth of July barbeque on our town square. I've got patrol this evening, but I've already checked to make sure my 'loose' uniform is clean and I'm going to fill up on barbeque before I start my shift."

Detective Scala said, "A man after my own heart. Up here, we have a thing called Taste of Chicago where a bunch of local restaurants serve food in one of our parks. I've already got some shorts and a tee shirt on and I'm good to go just as soon as I finish talking to you."

After saying, "Have a good holiday, and I'll give you a call as soon as I talk to Cairn Dumont," Dan Arthur hung up the phone.

Then he picked up the last message slip and dialed the number of the Las Vegas Police Department.

CHAPTER 119

"Detective bureau, Rayburn speaking."

"Detective Rayburn, this is Officer Dan Arthur Truman of the Delta City Arkansas Police Department. I understand you called Chief Laird. I'm covering for him this week, how can I help you?"

"Officer Truman, I've got a strange death and it looks like it might be connected to a couple of your citizens."

Dan Arthur asked, "So what have you got?"

"The victim's birth name is Buford Donaldson, but he's used enough aliases to fill a phone book. We've popped him a couple of times in the past for different kinds of cons but never could make anything stick."

Dan Arthur laughed and said, "The joys of police work."

"You got it. Anyway, we got a tip he had been involved in an armed robbery a couple of weeks back where a couple of people got shot. Early Tuesday morning one of our informants tipped us that Donaldson had just checked into a local hotel, so we got ready to take him down. When our SWAT team got inside the room, they found Donaldson dead. On his lap were papers showing where a Nicole Bailey of Delta City had gotten a divorce from Andrew James."

Dan Arthur said, "I know Nicole. She got divorced from Andrew James just about the time I joined the force so I didn't have any contact with him, but I know he took several of our citizens for quite a bit of money."

Detective Rayburn said, "We didn't have an 'Andrew James' AKA on Donaldson, but we knew that he had used 'James Andrews' for a while." With a laugh, he continued, "And despite what you beat cops think, even a detective could figure out that 'Andrew James' was probably one of Donaldson's aliases."

Dan Arthur laughed and said, "Delta City is so small we don't even have detectives. We rent them from the state police when we need one, but they've always done a pretty good job for us."

"Out here in Vegas it's a running battle between the silver shields and the gold shields. Okay, a quick examination of Buford Donaldson's body didn't show an obvious cause of death, so with the divorce papers on his lap and all we just chalked it up as some sort of suicide. Sometimes even the worst scumbag actually loves somebody."

Dan Arthur asked, "Do you want me to make a notification call to Nicole Bailey?"

"I wish it was that simple. All I needed to close the case was the ME's report, which came in this morning. But despite the big bucks we give them, the people over at the medical examiner's office couldn't find out why Donaldson died. He was in good health and didn't have any drugs in him, he just died."

Dan Arthur said, "Sounds like it might be a good time for ya'll to haul out that 'What happens in Vegas stays in Vegas' thing."

"Really. But there's actually another reason why I called you. Before SWAT did the takedown in the hotel, we evacuated all of the nearby rooms, and it turns out the room right next to where we found Donaldson had been occupied by a Donald Taylor, also of Delta City."

Dan Arthur said, "This is similar to some other stuff that's been happening involving Delta City folks. I'm going to be doing several interviews tomorrow, so can you put your people off until I finish them?"

Detective Rayburn said, "Yeah that will work okay. We're pretty much shut down for the holiday anyway."

Dan Arthur said, "Same here. I'll call you tomorrow afternoon."

Putting down the phone, Dan Arthur leaned back in the desk chair and said, "Shit."

CHAPTER 120

Dan Arthur was not the only person in Delta City who was burning up the telephone lines that Fourth of July morning. When Barbara awoke shortly before nine a.m., she immediately called Cairn.

"So what's up, Barbara? Did you and Dan Arthur take care of some official business last night?"

Barbara said, "Yeah, we did. You remember you told me you didn't totally believe in witchcraft, but that you didn't totally disbelieve in it either. Well, the other night when we were doing our incantations and shit I was aiming my spells at David Henson."

"Was that the guy in Monroe who beat you up and raped you?"

Barbara replied, "Yeah. He was found dead Monday morning and the medical examiners can't figure out why he died. That's what Dan Arthur wanted to talk to me about."

"Calm down, it's probably just a coincidence."

Barbara said, "Maybe, but it's a coincidence that hits a little too close to home for me. Dan Arthur was also asking me about a guy named Donnie Taylor."

Cairn asked, "Who's that?"

"Dan Arthur said he's some guy who's been following the Surfer Girls around since we were in high school. Supposedly, this Donnie Taylor has some kind of thing for us, and he was only a few blocks away from him when David Henson died."

Cairn said, "I don't know if it's witchcraft or not, but it does sound like something weird is going on. Have you talked to Nicole?"

Barbara said "No."

And Cairn responded, "Good, and let's leave her out of this until we find out a little more about what's going on. I've got to go set up my booth on the square, so why don't you come down and hang out with me. You know Dan Arthur will be coming over there for some of Mike's barbeque, so let's make ourselves easy targets. If Dan Arthur wants to talk to us he'll come by my booth, and if he doesn't we'll figure everything is okay."

Barbara said, "Sounds good to me. We'll just make it another day of acting normal. Oh, by the way, I fucked Dan Arthur after he was finished talking to me last night. Do you think that might help keep us out of jail?"

Cairn laughed and said, "I don't know, how good were you? See you on the square in a couple of hours."

CHAPTER 121

Shortly before noon, Dan Arthur forced a smile as he walked past the police dispatcher. Saying, "Happy Fourth, I'll see you later," he walked out of the police department and crossed the street to the town square.

Of course, it was purely by accident that when Dan Arthur entered the square he was right in front of the Mike's Restaurant booth, and since he was standing right there it would only make sense for him to go ahead and pick up a barbeque sandwich and a Coke to get warmed up with.

Having made a start on filling his stomach, Dan Arthur figured he could do a little police work. He looked across the square and saw Cairn's booth in its usual location. Noticing that Barbara was also standing there he thought, "*Two birds with one stone*," and started walking toward the booth.

CHAPTER 122

Cairn's booth was something she had started right after she returned to Delta City from New Mexico. Every Fourth of July she would set up three large sheets of plywood connected together with hinges to make a wall, and there she would hang some of her more modestly priced paintings. In front of the wall, she would set up an easel and make charcoal drawings of people attending the barbeque for five dollars each.

Cairn kept the proceeds from her painting sales, but the money from the charcoal drawings was split among several Delta City charities.

She wasn't especially imbued with public spiritedness, but Delta City was her home, and Cairn felt that if the people there could enjoy some of her work it was a good thing, and the money that went to charity made it even better.

Seeing Dan Arthur approaching, Barbara walked toward him and said, "Hi, Dan Arthur."

Smiling but keeping his voice in a neutral tone, Dan Arthur replied, "Hello, Barbara."

Leaning close and speaking quietly Barbara asked, "Is there any chance of you coming by my house after you finish your patrol tonight?"

"Barbara, I would really like to do that, but I can't. There have been three unexplained deaths recently that have some connection to the Surfer Girls, and I don't think we should take things any further until these incidents are resolved." Gently pressing Barbara's arm to direct her, he said, "Let's walk over to Cairn's booth so I can talk to both of you together."

When they reached the booth Cairn said, "Hi, Dan Arthur. Do you want me to draw you today? I can make you look really sexy."

Dan Arthur managed a tight smile as he said, "Even you aren't that good an artist, Cairn."

In a serious tone he said, "I'm afraid I'm going to have to have an official conversation with you and Barbara tomorrow. I'm guessing you two probably talked earlier, and that Barbara told you about the unexplained death of David Henson."

Looking at both women, Dan Arthur continued, "There have also been two other mysterious deaths, Jared DeCosta, whom I believe you knew, Cairn, and Andrew James, who was one of Nicole's husbands. I've been in law enforcement long enough to know that coincidences can occur, but I also know that when things like this do happen it is probably not just a coincidence."

"I want to talk to both of you at ten o'clock tomorrow morning. If you'd like, we can do the interviews at the police station, and you can bring a lawyer with you if you want to. Or, the three of us can meet at Cairn's house and I'll make it an informal chat for as long as I possibly can. I really don't think ya'll are involved in any criminal activities, although I may need to talk to you about that freezer in your shed, Cairn."

Dan Arthur could see both women's jaws drop, and he said, "I would prefer that we have an informal meeting at Cairn's house but I will need for both of you to be absolutely straight with me. And if I think you aren't, we'll have to move to the police department."

Barbara asked, "Do you want Nicole there, too?"

Dan Arthur said, "I'll leave it up to you for now, but I have the feeling that it might be best if we start our discussion without her."

Allowing his voice to take on a more pleasant tone, he said, "Now, I'm going to walk over to Mike's booth and have a couple of barbeque sandwiches. After I finish them I'll come back over here and you can tell me where you want to meet."

CHAPTER 123

Shortly before three o'clock Dan Arthur pulled on his "loose" uniform pants and noticing that they weren't quite as loose as they once were, he made a vow to hit the gym a little more often.

Since almost everyone in Delta City was at the barbeque, Dan Arthur could allow his mind to wander as he made his patrol rounds.

He was pleased that Barbara and Cairn had agreed to meet with him at Cairn's house. Even though he knew that something was going on, as evidenced by the three deaths, he hoped he could find a way to quietly resolve the matter.

For some reason, the day Bobby Ellis died kept elbowing its way into his memory.

Like most cops, Dan Arthur had seen more than his share of strange things. He'd been to many a house to investigate strange noises heard by the elderly occupants, and he'd stood in more than one pasture while a farmer pointed out what he believed was a UFO. While he'd usually been able to find an explanation for the noises or UFO's, a few things had remained in the unexplained column.

Dan Arthur had known Bobby Ellis, even though he hadn't especially cared for him, and after Bobby had pulled his stunt with the "witch's tit" comment and grabbing Barbara's breasts Dan Arthur had liked him even less.

He hadn't been at Mike's Restaurant the day Bobby Ellis died, but he knew all about it. He'd heard how Barbara and Cairn were chanting their witchcraft incantations, and how Nicole was flashing her tits when Bobby pulled out in front of the truck that killed him.

But Dan Arthur had played football with Bobby, and knew that he was a guy who wasn't easily rattled. Even if all three of the Surfer Girls had their tits out Dan Arthur didn't think it would have been enough to distract Bobby so much that he would pull out in front of a truck.

And while the universe frequently offers numerous explanations as to why things happen, if it came down to choosing between witchcraft and Nicole's boobs as the reason for Bobby's death, Dan Arthur wasn't one hundred per cent sure that he would go with the tit flash explanation.

As far as the three recent deaths went, there was another common element besides the Surfer Girls: Donnie Taylor. But while Dan Arthur sometimes thought that Donnie was a little bit creepy, he couldn't see him killing anyone, even if all three of the Surfer Girls were naked and on bended knee begging him to.

Dan Arthur had already figured out how he was going to handle Donnie Taylor. Delta City Appliance World would open at nine o'clock tomorrow morning, and Dan Arthur felt he would know everything he needed to know from Donnie by 9:10.

CHAPTER 124

When Dan Arthur entered Delta City Appliance World, Donnie Taylor's mother warmly greeted him, saying, "Dan Arthur, how are you? I think Donnie found you a big screen at the electronics show. He's in the back, let me call him." She picked up the phone, paged him, and a couple of seconds later Donnie came to the front of the store.

"Dan Arthur, I think I found the perfect TV for you when I was in Las Vegas."

Dan Arthur smiled and said, "Great! Tell you what, it's such a nice morning, why don't we sit on the square while you tell me about it?"

As they sat down on one of the concrete benches on the town square, Dan Arthur said, "Donnie, you can tell me about the TV later. Something's come up and I need to talk to you on an official basis."

Donnie laughed and said, "That seems to be all I'm doing lately. Everywhere I've been this week I've ended up talking to the cops, sorry, I mean 'the police'."

Dan Arthur said, "So I've heard," and noticed that Donnie flinched.

"Donnie, I'm not going to play any 'good cop, bad cop' or other games on you. Three people are dead for no apparent reason, one in Monroe, one in Chicago, and one in Las Vegas. You weren't very far away when each of these people died, and all of them had some kind of connection to the Surfer Girls."

Dan Arthur could tell that Donnie was very visibly rattled, and said, "I don't really think you or the Surfer Girls were involved in any of these deaths, so I'd like to put this whole thing to rest as soon as possible. To do that, I'm going to ask you some questions. Some of them may hurt your feelings, and I'm sorry about that. But you need to answer me truthfully, and you don't need to bullshit me to try to protect the Surfer Girls, because I promise you that I don't think they need protecting. Do we have a deal?"

Donnie nodded, and Dan Arthur asked, "Who is David Henson?"

Donnie said, "I don't know him. Is he one of the people…?"

Dan Arthur cut him off, saying, "We don't need to go into details right now. Who is Bobby Ellis?"

Donnie said, "I knew a Bobby Ellis in high school. He got killed in a car wreck."

Dan Arthur nodded and said, "Who is Jared DeCosta?"

"I don't know him."

"Who is Delbert McGraw?"

Donnie said, "Wasn't he Nicole's first husband?"

"Who is Bryan Selig?"

"I think he was Barbara's boyfriend in high school."

"Who is Andrew James?"

"He was Nicole's third husband. He stole a bunch of money from people here in Delta City."

Dan Arthur said, "One more, who is Chuckie Howard?"

Donnie looked puzzled for a second, then said, "Was he that stoner kid when we were in high school?"

"Okay, you're doing fine, Donnie. Now remember that you promised to be straight with me. In the past week, have you taken any actions that might have resulted in the death of someone?"

Donnie thought for a moment, and then said, "I blew a stop sign in Monroe."

Dan Arthur said, "That's it?"

"That's it."

"Donnie, did any of the Surfer Girls ask you to take any action that might have resulted in the death of someone?"

Donnie didn't say anything for several seconds, then his face seemed to crumple as he said, "Dan Arthur, we both know that the Surfer Girls never see me even when I'm standing right next to them. None of them has ever talked to me except one time in high school when Barbara dropped her books and I helped her pick them up. But when she thanked me she got my name wrong."

Donnie looked like he was about to cry, and Dan Arthur felt sorry for him. Donnie might be a little creepy, but other than his infatuation with the Surfer Girls, he wasn't a bad guy. And Dan Arthur was sure that this was the first time Donnie had acknowledged his invisibility to the Surfer Girls, even to himself.

In a sympathetic voice he said, "Donnie, I'm truly sorry that I had to put you through that, and I want you to know that I will never tell anybody about this conversation. Okay?"

Donnie nodded his head in affirmation, and Dan Arthur said, "You know, if you'd give Sue Carol Raines a chance you might like her better as herself than when she's pretending to be a Surfer Girl." With a smile, Dan Arthur added, "And just think about how much gas money you'd save if you quit following the Surfer Girls around all of the time."

Donnie managed a faint smile as he said, "Thanks, Dan Arthur. Maybe I'll see if Sue Carol wants to go to a movie or something tonight."

CHAPTER 125

Opening the door in response to Dan Arthur's knock, Cairn said, "We're in the kitchen. Come on in and I'll get you a cup of coffee."

Barbara was sitting at the kitchen table and she managed a wan smile as she said, "Hello, Dan Arthur."

Taking the cup of coffee from Cairn, Dan Arthur sat down and said, "Morning, Barbara."

Dan Arthur said, "I want you to know that I don't like having to question you like this, but I try to be a good cop, and to do that sometimes I have to do things I don't enjoy. But like I told you yesterday, there are three dead men out there, and when each of them was found, there was a piece of paper lying next to them that would tie them directly back to one of you or to Nicole. They found one man in Monroe, another in Chicago, and the third one in Las Vegas. They have fine detectives in each of those cities, and it's just a matter of time before they come knocking at your doors. And I don't think any of us want that."

Barbara said, "No shit!" which brought her a rebuking glance from Cairn.

"I don't think any of you were involved in these deaths, since all of you were here in Delta City when they happened. But whether you were or weren't, I need for you to be straight with me, and if you do that, I'll do my best to help you out. We've been friends for a long time and I'd like for us to still be friends when all of this is over."

Cairn said, "Barbara and I talked it over. We know you've got a job to do and we won't hold anything against you."

Dan Arthur said, "I hoped you would understand. Now, I'm going to start asking ya'll some questions. If either of you say anything that might could put you in some kind of legal jeopardy I'll forget what you said, but I'll have to end this conversation. I'll advise you to get a lawyer and you will need to come down to the station. Also, I have to tell you that if I think either of you aren't being straight with me I'll do the same thing. Now, you might find some of my questions a little embarrassing, but you'll have to live with it. Agreed?"

In unison, Barbara and Cairn said, "Agreed."

Consulting his notebook, Dan Arthur said, "Victim number one was David Henson in Monroe. Barbara, I believe you said he beat you up and raped you."

Barbara said, "That's correct."

Cairn interjected, "I saw the pictures where she had a black eye and a split lip."

Dan Arthur said, "Okay. Victim number two was Jared. Cairn, the detective in Chicago told me he talked to a woman named Linda Devinie, and she said you were doing a lot of cocaine back when you lived up there. Ms. Devinie said something about this DeCosta promising you a promotion to get you into bed, but that he left town the next day. Is that about it?"

Cairn quietly replied, "Yes. Dan Arthur, when I moved to Chicago after I finished art school it was a whole different world. Everybody was doing cocaine all the time at the ad agency where I worked. I couldn't afford to buy all of the coke I wanted, so I ended up sleeping with men who would give it to me. I tried to rationalize it as being like Nicole sleeping with men she thought had money, but it really wasn't like that. If I wasn't actually a coke whore, I wasn't far from it. The thing with Jared happened pretty much the way you described it. And I swear to you, I haven't done any cocaine since I left Chicago except for one time."

Dan Arthur gave a brief smile, then said, "Cairn, I know just about every person in Delta City who does any kind of drugs, and I know what drugs they're doing. But as long as they aren't selling anything and do their jobs and take care of their families or whatever, I don't feel compelled to run them in for what they do in the privacy of their own homes."

He glanced at his notebook and continued, "Victim number three was Nicole's third husband, Andrew James, and I think everybody in Delta City knows what kind of person he was. They found him dead in Las Vegas."

Barbara tried to stifle a laugh as she said, "Poor Nicole."

Dan Arthur smiled and said, "Her luck with men ain't exactly been the best, has it? Now I think just about anybody would agree that these three guys were all lowlifes, but that doesn't give people the right to go around killing them."

"Now, I told Barbara about Donnie Taylor. He's been in love with all of the Surfer Girls since high school. Did she mention him to you, Cairn?"

"Barbara said something about him, but I still don't have the slightest idea who he is."

Dan Arthur said, "To tell you the truth, I really don't remember him from high school either. Anyway, Donnie just happened to have the bad luck to be near where each of these deaths occurred right around the time they happened. At first I thought there was a slight possibility that ya'll might have asked him to get rid of these three guys, or that he might have just decided to do it on his own since he had such a thing for the Surfer Girls. He knew who Andrew James was, course everybody in Delta City knows about him. But he told me he'd never heard of David Henson or Jared DeCosta, and I believe him. By the way, I don't think he'll be following ya'll around anymore."

Barbara laughed and said, "I don't think that will really matter since we never knew he was following us around in the first place."

Dan Arthur shook his head and said, "Poor Donnie. He's really a pretty nice guy, just a little misguided."

Putting a serious tone in his voice, Dan Arthur said, "Okay, let's cut to the chase. Were either of you two or Nicole involved in the deaths of the three men I mentioned?"

Barbara and Cairn exchanged glances, then Barbara quietly said, "We aren't sure."

After just sitting there for a few moments, Dan Arthur said, "If it was anybody else that told me that I'd just take them in and let the district attorney sort things out. But if ya'll want to expand on that I'll be happy to listen."

Barbara said, "You remember how back in high school we messed with witchcraft for a few months?"

Dan Arthur said, "Some people in Delta City believe that it was your witchcraft that killed Bobby Ellis after he groped Barbara."

Barbara looked startled and said, "You better tell the next part, Cairn."

Cairn took a deep breath, and then said, "Dan Arthur, you said something about the freezer in my backyard shed. Did you look inside it?"

Dan Arthur said, "Officially, no. But when I was investigating the disappearance of that car thief a while back, I saw something unusual on the recording from my patrol car's dashboard camera. I thought it was kinda strange that the lights would be on in your shed in the middle of the night and then go off, so I decided to do a little snooping. Of course, since I didn't have a warrant I can't use whatever I saw out there against you in court, but if I need to, I can figure out a way to get a warrant."

Cairn nodded her head and said, "I understand. Now I'm not saying you saw anything, but if you did see a dead body in the freezer it might be because I picked him up outside the University Club and brought him home with me."

Dan Arthur said, "If I saw something."

Cairn said, "Right. Anyway, if I did bring a man home, maybe that was the one time I've done any cocaine since I left Chicago."

Dan Arthur nodded his head as Cairn continued, "And maybe if I brought a man home I was going to go to bed with him, but maybe he pushed things a little too fast. Maybe I was a little bit paranoid from the cocaine and maybe I bit down on what he had stuck in my mouth."

Barbara grinned as Dan Arthur involuntarily flinched, and Cairn continued, "And maybe if I did bite the man he might have jumped back and hit his head on the dresser and died."

"And if the dead man happened to end up in your freezer, could that have been Barbara's idea?"

Cairn said, "No, it was Nicole who first came up with it. She was talking about something she saw on Law & Order where the Mafia whacked some guy and put him in a meat cooler. Then Barbara said…wait, then maybe Barbara could have suggested that we put the dead guy in the freezer until we figured out what to do next."

Dan Arthur nodded and said, "That sounds like an accidental death to me. I imagine the district attorney would just ignore the fact that you failed to report the death since ya'll were scared."

Cairn sighed with relief, and Dan Arthur said, "So how does what might have happened between Cairn and the guy in the freezer fit with what did happen to David Henson, Jared DeCosta, and Andrew James?"

Barbara said, "Well, you know how Nicole is when she gets drunk. We were sitting around the University Club one night a week or so later and she says something about seeing Randy Davis a couple of days earlier and starts babbling about when we were witches in high school."

Dan Arthur asked, "Is that the boy Nicole claimed raped her in high school?"

Barbara said, "That's him. Then she started going on about how we had killed Bobby Ellis with witchcraft and how Cairn killed the car thief, and how we ought to use witchcraft to kill some of the other men who'd fucked up our lives. We told her that Bobby Ellis got killed because Nicole flashed her boobs at him and he got distracted and pulled out in front of that truck, and that Cairn had killed the car thief by accident, but Nicole didn't want to hear it."

Cairn quickly interjected, "Not that we're saying that I killed him."

Dan Arthur grinned and nodded his head in affirmation, and Barbara continued, "Anyway, Nicole had made up her mind that we were going to kill some guys with witchcraft and that was that. So Cairn and I figured 'what the hell' and decided to go along with Nicole to shut her up."

Cairn picked up the story, saying, "Then me and Barbara had to go back through all of our bad memories to decide who should die. Last Friday night we got together over at Nicole's and did some incantations and cast some spells to try to kill these guys, and now we find out they all died right after that."

Dan Arthur asked, "And that's the whole story?"

Barbara said, "That's it. And we both swear to God that it's the honest truth."

Dan Arthur leaned back in his chair and said, "Let me think about this for a few minutes."

Cairn said, "I'll get us some more coffee," and after she refilled the cups, everyone sat in silence.

Finally, Dan Arthur leaned forward and said, "We have two possibilities here. One, these three men died from something other than witchcraft, but the medical examiners just haven't found the reasons yet. If that's the case, and ya'll weren't involved, there's really not a problem. But it's hard for me to believe that out of four different medical examiners, not one can find a cause of death."

"The second possibility is that these men died because ya'll put spells on them. And to tell you the truth, I'd always wondered about that thing with Bobby Ellis. Bobby wasn't the kind of guy to get distracted, even by Nicole's tits, and with all of the girls he was screwing, I'm sure it wasn't the first pair he'd ever seen. I'm not saying that I absolutely believe these men died because of your witchcraft, I'm just saying I don't absolutely believe they didn't."

Cairn quietly said, "Bobby had his foot on the brake. I could see how tense his body was from trying to stop and I heard him scream as his car moved forward. I don't know if it was witchcraft or not, but something unseen pushed Bobby's car out in front of that truck."

Barbara said, "I always thought the witchcraft thing was just a silly goof, but we put spells on three guys and now they're dead, so it's hard for me to not believe that something supernatural is going on."

Everyone sat quietly for a few moments, then Dan Arthur said, "There's a possibility I can handle this in such a way that it will all just simply go away, but the only way that can happen is if we can keep the whole thing a secret."

"Before I started talking to you two about this situation, did any of you know who the other two had decided to put a spell on?"

Barbara said, "I guess both Cairn and I could have guessed that Nicole would pick Andrew James since he fucked her over so bad. And since Cairn and I have talked to each other about a lot of stuff she might have been able to guess that I would pick David Henson and I probably could have figured out that she would pick Jared DeCosta. But since Nicole didn't know about any of that stuff she wouldn't have been able to know who Cairn and I had picked."

Dan Arthur said, "So there's no way any of you could have absolutely known who the others had picked? You didn't say their names as part of your rituals or whatever?"

Barbara said, "Each of us had written the name down on a little piece of paper. Nicole had put some ashtrays out and as part of casting the spell we each lit our piece of paper on fire and let it burn up in an ashtray. And none of us saw the other people's piece of paper."

Dan Arthur smiled and said, "Somehow plain old ashtrays didn't fit with my picture of casting spells."

Cairn indignantly said, "Well, they were black ashtrays, plastic ones that Nicole stole from the University Club."

Dan Arthur said, "Okay, calm down Cairn, I'm just teasing. Now, the only way I can bury this is if I know that none of you are ever going to talk about this to anyone under any circumstances. I think the two of you are smart enough to keep your mouths shut, but frankly, I'm worried about Nicole. It's no secret that when she gets drunk she sometimes develops a severe case of diarrhea of the mouth. Right now, Nicole doesn't know that Andrew James is dead and I think I can keep her from hearing about it until after this has all blown over, but we have to figure out some way of handling her for the long term. Anybody have any ideas?"

Cairn brightly said, "We could try putting a spell on her, and maybe make her lose her memory."

Dan Arthur almost yelled, "No, absolutely not! If I handle this, I will have to have your solemn promises that there will be no more witchcraft and no more spells put on anyone, for any reason. Is that clear?"

Cairn meekly replied, "Absolutely clear. It was just an idea."

Barbara quietly said, "We can't make Nicole lose her memory, but maybe we can fix it so nobody pays any attention to what she says."

Dan Arthur said, "Go on."

Barbara continued, "Nicole is going to Mexico on Monday for a two-week vacation. There are some really gossipy people who work at the hospital with me, and suppose they heard that Nicole hadn't really gone on vacation. Suppose they heard that Nicole had finally gone off the deep end and that she had gone somewhere for a little mental health tune up. It wouldn't be but a couple of hours before the story was all over town. And since Nicole talks enough wild shit already, if people thought she had a few screws loose they wouldn't pay any attention to anything she said about anything."

Dan Arthur asked, "You don't think that's a little bit extreme?"

Barbara said, "Look, if Bobby Ellis died because of witchcraft, it was just a stupid high school thing. We didn't really think our spells would actually work. And if Cairn was involved in the car thief's death it was totally an accident. But this whole thing we're dealing with now with the witchcraft and the three dead guys came out of Nicole's twisted brain. If Cairn and I had thought that our witch shit would really work we wouldn't have done it. We only went along with it to shut Nicole up. But who knows what other wacky shit she might come up with, and who she might be able to talk into going along with it. Giving Nicole the reputation of being a little bit nuts might turn out to be a good way of preventing any other shit like this in the future."

Cairn said, "I hate to say it, but that does kinda make sense."

Dan Arthur said, "I guess it does. I'm sure there are a few guys around who would do just about anything to get into Nicole's pants."

Barbara said, "Like, what's his name, Donnie Taylor."

Dan Arthur laughed and said, "I think poor Donnie's puppy-dog devotion to the Surfer Girls has finally come to an end, but he's hardly the only nutcase we have here in Delta City."

Barbara quietly asked, "So I should get the rumor mill going on Monday?"

Both Cairn and Dan Arthur nodded their affirmation, then Dan Arthur said, "Okay, now that we've taken care of the witchcraft thing we still have one other situation to deal with, namely Cairn's freezer."

He continued, "When somebody dies from other than natural causes, cops like to do their job, find the bad guy, and wrap the whole thing up in a neat little package. But sometimes the dead guy is such a bad person that we really don't give a shit that he's dead, and we aren't really interested in busting our asses to get out the ribbon and bows. That car thief, Terry Hardin, was one of those really bad people, and if nothing turns up regarding whoever killed him, the case will probably be quickly backburnered, and will eventually end up in the bottom of a never-opened file drawer."

"So, when I leave here, I'm going to go to the police station and make a couple of phone calls. One of them will be to try to make your little witchcraft shit go away. The other will be to find out how active the Terry Hardin case is."

Changing to a friendlier tone, Dan Arthur broadly winked and said, "Now Cairn, I believe you told me that you have a broken down freezer out in your shed that you'd like to have hauled off."

Cairn said, "Uh, I really don't remember saying…"

Barbara cut Cairn off and said, "That's right Dan Arthur. She doesn't need it anymore and just wants to get rid of it."

Dan Arthur smiled and said, "Good, I've got an idea how to handle that problem, and if the Terry Hardin case is as dead as I think it is, we'll get together tomorrow morning and take care of it."

Cairn said, "Thank you, Dan Arthur."

"You might want to hold off on that 'thank you', Cairn. If this whole thing doesn't go down the way we want it to, the Surfer Girls might have to deal with some out-of-town detectives digging around in their lives, and you might have to answer a few questions about the freezer, but I really don't think any of you will face any serious legal problems."

"But I'm in a different situation. If anybody ever found out that I helped ya'll out I would lose my job and probably go to jail. So, here's the deal. I have pictures showing what's in the freezer, that the freezer is in the shed, and that the shed is in Cairn's back yard. They're my insurance policy. If anybody does anything that makes this thing fall apart, we'll all be going down together. I hate to do this since we've been friends for a long time, but I hope you understand the risks I'm taking to save your asses."

Barbara said, "We understand, and we really appreciate what you're doing for us."

Standing up, Dan Arthur said, "I'm going to go make my phone calls. Barbara, why don't you give me your cell phone number. I'll give you a buzz in a couple of hours and let you know what's happening with the freezer."

CHAPTER 126

After letting Dan Arthur out, Cairn came back into the kitchen and said, "You must have really fucked his brains out, Barbara!"

Barbara said, "I don't think that had anything to do with it. I think it's just like Dan Arthur said, that we've been friends for a long time. Plus, Dan Arthur is a pragmatist, and he knows that sometimes police work is more than just enforcing the law."

Cairn said, "Well, whatever. I do feel kinda bad about us throwing Nicole under the train."

"And what do you think would have happened if the situation had been reversed? Do you really think Nicole would have put her ass on the line for us? I don't feel great about making Nicole out to be nuts, but face it, she's been heading that way for quite a while now. I'm just going to rationalize it as restating the obvious."

Cairn asked, "Do you think I'm nuts, believing in all of that witchcraft stuff?"

Barbara replied, "With three dead guys out there, maybe I'm the one who's nuts for not believing in it."

CHAPTER 127

As Dan Arthur drove toward the police department building he glanced toward Café on the Square and saw Lee Mitchell's State Police car parked in front. Thinking, "*This will save me a phone call,*" he parked his car and hurried across the street toward the café.

The state policeman was seated at the counter, and Dan Arthur took the stool next to him, saying, "Hello, Lee."

"Hi, Dan Arthur. They keeping you busy?"

"Driving me crazy, Lee. Chief Laird's brother is sick, and he's been over in Shreveport taking care of him for the last week."

Lee laughed and said, "And I'll bet the city isn't giving you a dime for all of the extra work you're doing."

"Dime, hell! Not even a penny!"

Lee said, "Well, at least you're getting plenty of training for when you get a chief's job."

Dan Arthur laughed and said, "God forbid! Covering for Chief Laird has only reminded me how much I don't want to be a chief. If I have my way, I'll be driving a patrol car right up until the day I retire!"

Lee asked, "How's Chief Laird's brother doing?"

Dan Arthur replied, "Not so good. Last time I talked to Chief Laird he said it's pretty much touch-and-go at this point."

"Sorry to hear that. Give Chief Laird my sympathy, will you?"

Dan Arthur said, "Will do." Quickly checking his notebook, he said, "Lee, I'm trying to get some of the paperwork off my desk while I'm hanging around the station. What ever happened with that Terry Harding who left the stolen Mercedes in the University Club parking lot?"

Lee laughed and said, "Looks like he may have just dropped off the face of the earth. At least that's what I hope happened. Last time I talked to Dallas they said they had a lead on him in Los Angeles, but it didn't pan out, and as far as I'm concerned it's Texas' problem. The file on Harding is at the bottom of the pile on my desk."

Dan Arthur smiled and said, "I'm thinking about just stuffing mine into the cold case drawer."

Lee said, "That works for me. I'll let you know if the case goes hot again."

Draining his coffee cup, Dan Arthur said, "I'd better be getting back across the street. The way my luck's going we probably had a whole crime wave get started while I was sitting here."

The state policeman laughed and said, "See you later," as Dan Arthur walked out the door.

CHAPTER 128

Walking back to the police department, Dan Arthur pulled out his cell phone and dialed.

"Barbara, this is Dan Arthur. I'll meet you and Cairn tomorrow morning at ten o'clock at her house and we can deal with the freezer thing then."

Barbara replied, "Okay, we'll see you tomorrow."

CHAPTER 129

Dan Arthur had avoided a phone call to the State Police by his fortuitous meeting with Officer Lee Mitchell at Café on the Square, but there was another phone call to be made and he was not looking forward to it.

He tried to decide what he was going to say as he shuffled papers around on the chief's desk, looking for the instructions for making a four-way conference call. Somehow, he didn't think the three detectives he would be speaking with would buy something like, "*Well, guys, your unexplained deaths are the result of some of my citizens doing a little witchcraft.*"

But after a couple of more minutes of thought, Dan Arthur came up with the words he was looking for and began dialing the phone to set up the conference call.

CHAPTER 130

Speaking into the phone, Dan Arthur said, "Why don't ya'll introduce yourselves and we can get started."

"This is Detective Bobby Joe McDonald with the Monroe, Louisiana Police Department."

"Detective Vince Rayburn with the Las Vegas PD."

"Detective Angie Scala, Chicago Police Department."

"Thank you," said Dan Arthur. "Just so everybody knows what's going on, let me recite the details. Each of you has a dead body, and none of your medical examiners has been able to find a cause of death for your victims. Some evidence found at each death scene ties the victim back to one of three women who live here in Delta City. And right around the time of each death, one of my citizens named Donald Taylor was in the vicinity."

Vince Rayburn said, "I suppose it would be too much to hope that you have all of the perps in custody and all we need to do is come pick them up."

Dan Arthur laughed and said, "Oh hell yeah! Got 'em all locked up in my jail. Ya'll just come on down and take your pick."

As the other men joined in the laughter Dan Arthur said, "I wish it was that simple."

Detective Scala said, "Excuse me for interrupting, but did you say that there are three of these unexplained deaths that somehow tie back to Delta City?"

"That's correct. And as ya'll requested, I've interviewed most of the Delta City citizens that have come up in your investigations so I've got a little more information to add. The three women are all friends, and they've been called the Surfer Girls since they were in high school. I spoke with two of them, and it turns out that David Henson from Monroe had raped one of them when she was in college, and Jared DeCosta of Chicago had promised the other woman a promotion if she slept with him, then ran out on the deal. I didn't talk to the third woman, but she was once married to Andrew James, the Las Vegas victim. Andrew James stole a lot of money from people here in Delta City, which led to a lot of public embarrassment for his then wife. All three of your victims were pretty much scumbags, at least around the time the Surfer Girls were involved with them."

Detective Rayburn said "Sounds like we've got motive for all three of these women, which leaves us with means and opportunity."

Dan Arthur said, "Based on the evidence, it would appear that some type of poison or drugs might have been the cause of death. One of the Surfer Girls works at our local hospital, but she's a physical therapist so I doubt that she had access to any sort of drugs, although anything is possible."

"But the whole thing falls apart on opportunity. All of the Surfer Girls were right here in Delta City when these men died. I saw a couple of the women myself, and I'm sure plenty of other people saw all three of them."

Detective McDonald asked, "Officer Truman, didn't you tell me that this Donald Taylor had some kind of thing for the Surfer Girls? Is it possible they might have put him up to killing our victims, or that he did it on his own as some sort of gift?"

Dan Arthur said, "That crossed my mind, too. Donnie was near the scenes when the deaths occurred, so he would be a likely suspect. But he owns a local appliance store, and he had told me before the fact that he was going to Monroe Sunday to spend the night and catch an early flight to Chicago the next morning. He was going to some kind of appliance dealer's show there. After that, he was going to fly to Las Vegas and spend Monday night there, then go to an electronics show on Tuesday."

Detective McDonald said, "He did tell my officer that the reason he was speeding was because he didn't want to be late for his flight, and the road he was pulled over on is a shortcut to the Monroe airport."

Detective Scala added, "The appliance show was going on that day and my officer encountered him in a logical place for someone catching the EL to O'Hare airport to be."

Detective Rayburn said, "We were having an electronics dealers show the day Donald Taylor was in Las Vegas, and it would have been just a short shuttle ride from the hotel where he was staying to the convention center."

Dan Arthur said, "So Donnie's story matches up, with him being where he said he was going to be when he said he was going to be there. When I interviewed him, Donnie told me that he wasn't involved in any of the killings and based on both the evidence and his demeanor during questioning I believe him."

Detective Rayburn said, "So, we're back to square zero."

Dan Arthur quietly said, "There is one more thing. The Surfer Girls provided one additional possibility when I interviewed them and I'm neither endorsing it nor rejecting it, but let me tell you that it's way out there."

Detective McDonald said, "Well, way out there is better than what we've got now, which is nothing. Might as well throw it out there, and see what sticks."

Dan Arthur said, "Nicole Bailey, the one who was married to Andrew James, late of Las Vegas, has a little bit of a drinking prob…scratch that. The only thing that keeps Nicole from being labeled the town drunk is all of the money her daddy has."

Detective McDonald laughed and said, "We've got a couple of those in Monroe, too."

Dan Arthur continued, "Sometime back Nicole ran into a fellow she'd had some bad history with in high school, and somehow she decided that the Surfer Girls ought to kill some of the men who'd treated them badly."

Detective Scala said, "Ah, the old a woman scorned thing. Some weekends we have so many of them that we don't even have enough room to lock them all up."

Dan Arthur took a deep breath, and said, "This is where we start hitting way out there territory. When they were in high school, the Surfer Girls played around with witchcraft for a couple of months and Nicole got it in her head that they should use witchcraft to get rid of the guys that had done them wrong. Last Friday night the Surfer Girls got together over at Nicole's house. They had each written down the name of one man, who turned out to be your victims. They did some chanting and cast some spells and whatever else witches do, and now these three guys are dead and nobody can figure out why."

There was a long silence, then Detective Rayburn said, "So, the Surfer Girls told you that they cast some spells on these guys and now they're dead. Is that about it?"

Dan Arthur said, "That's it. And I imagine you guys are about ready to start fitting everybody in Delta City for straitjackets, including me."

Detective Scala asked, "Officer Truman, what do you think about the Surfer Girls story?"

Dan Arthur said, "Damned if I know what to think about it."

There was another long silence, then Detective McDonald quietly said, "A few years back I worked on a joint investigation with the New Orleans Police Department. They were dealing with some unexplained deaths among some people who got mixed up with those folks who practice voodoo down there in the swamp and we never did figure out why those victims died."

Detective Scala said, "I have to admit we've had a few unexplained deaths show up in Chicago. Most of the time we were able to eventually figure them out, but we've still got a few open cases."

Detective Rayburn laughed and said, "Hell, here in Vegas we're not but a couple of hours from Area 51 and we've had a few weird things in our back yard over the years. Now let me throw something out here. I don't know how you guys do it in your cities, but here's how we do it in Las Vegas. Until the medical examiner comes up with a cause of death, if we don't have any viable suspects we just sit on the case, and after we've sat on it for a while we cold case it and let it go."

Detective McDonald said, "So, you think we should all just cold case these deaths?"

Detective Rayburn replied, "Let me ask you, do you want to go in and tell your chief what Officer Truman told us today?"

Detective McDonald said, "No fuckin' way!"

And Detective Scala said, "I'm not about to either!"

Dan Arthur said, "Then it appears we have a consensus to just let these sleeping dogs lie. Agreed?"

The three detectives answered in unison, "Agreed."

Dan Arthur said, "Detectives, it's been my pleasure to work with you on this. If you ever make it to Delta City the beer's on me. Hopefully the next time we talk it will be under better circumstances."

And after a round of goodbyes, everyone hung up.

CHAPTER 131

The next morning Dan Arthur backed his truck into Cairn's backyard and parked as close to the shed as he could. He had a two-wheel hand truck with him, and with the help of Barbara and Cairn, the freezer was soon loaded into the back of his truck.

Brushing the dust off her hands Barbara asked, "So what's next?"

Dan Arthur replied, "You and Cairn jump in the truck. We're going to take a ride out to Hilltop Used Auto Parts and have them run the freezer through their car crusher. We'll say we're doing it so some kid doesn't get trapped inside and smother. Those old boys who run Hilltop really don't want me checking out their stack of car titles and VIN number plates, so they'll do what I tell them to, and they'll keep quiet about it."

Cairn asked, "Do you really need us to go along? Don't they have some guys who could help you unload the freezer?"

Dan Arthur grinned and said, "You and Barbara are coming along so you'll be incriminated. I wasn't kidding when I said if I go down we all go down."

Barbara laughed and said, "All of this talk about going down is making me horny. Let's go do what we've got to do so we can all get back to normal."

After the trip to Hilltop Used Auto Parts was complete, Dan Arthur pulled his truck to the curb in front of Cairn's house to let the two women out.

Barbara said, "Go on in the house, Cairn. I need to talk to Dan Arthur."

As Cairn walked up her sidewalk, Barbara said, "Dan Arthur, is there any chance of you stopping by my house after work tonight?"

"Barbara, I'd really like to, but I think we better put things on hold for a few days until things settle down. After that we'll talk and see where we go from there."

Barbara looked disappointed, but said, "I suppose that's probably the best thing to do. Rain check?"

Dan Arthur smiled and said, "Rain check."

CHAPTER 132

When Dan Arthur arrived at the police station on Monday morning, he was pleased to see Harry Laird back in his chair in the chief's office.

"Hi, Chief, good to see you back!"

Chief Laird said, "Come on in, Dan Arthur, and bring me up to speed on what happened while I was gone."

Taking a chair, Dan Arthur said, "Things have really been pretty slow. The patrol officers had to drive a couple of fellows home after they drank too much at the Fourth of July barbeque, but that's about it. How's your brother?"

Chief Laird said, "I'm glad it was a quiet week for you. It looks like my brother's going to live, but he's going to need to have someone around to help take care of him."

"I'm glad he's going to make it. By the way, I saw Lee Mitchell and he sent his sympathy."

"Tell him I said thanks next time you see him." Chief Laird's face took on a troubled look and he said, "Dan Arthur, why don't you close the door so we can have a private conversation."

Dan Arthur was a little bit concerned as he closed the door, but he kept his tone light as he said, "So what's up, Chief?"

Chief Laird sat for a moment, then said, "Dan Arthur, I'm thinking about calling it quits. I'm the last family my brother has, and I kind of think I ought to be with him now."

Dan Arthur nodded his head and Chief Laird continued, "I've got a little place in Shreveport, that cabin I built on Cross Lake a few years ago. I talked to a fellow I know who used to be with the Springhill Police Department. He's got a detective agency in Shreveport, and he said if I got my P.I.'s license he'd throw a little work my way. With all of the years I've got in here in Delta City I'll qualify for a halfway decent pension, so I'm thinking about retiring."

"I understand, but I'd sure hate to see you go."

Chief Laird said, "I haven't made up my mind one hundred percent yet, but I'm going to think about it this morning. If I decide to go I'll meet with the mayor later today and let him know."

"Well don't think you're going to sneak out of here without us throwing a party for you!"

Chief Laird managed a smile and said, "I wouldn't miss it for the world. By the way, I stopped by the Monroe Police Department to visit with some of my friends on my way back. I had a nice chat with a Detective McDonald."

Dan Arthur thought, "*Oh shit!*"

"Detective McDonald had some really nice things to say about you, Dan Arthur. He said he'd been talking to you over the last few days about one of his cases and he said you're a damned good policeman, but more than that you're a damned good cop."

Dan Arthur barely contained a sigh of relief as he grinned and said, "You'll have my ears burning if you keep that up."

Chief Laird smiled and said, "I agree with him, and I'll bet every cop who's ever worked with you would say the same thing. Even Bigfoot."

Dan Arthur said, "Bigfoot was the best teacher a small-town cop could have. Truly one of a kind."

Chief Laird said, "Probably the best small town cop I've ever known. Well, now that I'm back there's really no need for you to hang around here this morning. I imagine you've got some things around your house that need to be done."

Dan Arthur said, "I don't even want to think about it."

Chief Laird laughed and said, "Do me a favor and keep your cell phone handy in case I need to get hold of you."

Dan Arthur smiled and said, "Will do, Chief!"

CHAPTER 133

It was a little after one o'clock and Dan Arthur was pulling some bed sheets out of the dryer when his cell phone rang.

"Dan Arthur? Chief Laird. A couple of things have come up. Can you meet me over at City Hall at two o'clock?"

Dan Arthur knew there was a regularly scheduled City Council meeting at that time, but since it was rarely necessary for him to attend, he wasn't sure what awaited him when he walked into City Hall.

He saw Chief Laird and the mayor engaged in what appeared to be a pleasant conversation, and relaxed slightly as he approached them.

The mayor smiled and said, "Dan Arthur, good to see you!"

Dan Arthur returned the smile and said, "Mister Mayor, Chief Laird."

The police chief said, "Dan Arthur, I turned in my retirement papers to the mayor a little while ago."

The mayor said, "I tried to give them back, but the chief insisted. I hate to see him go, but with what his brother's going through I understand why he needs to move to Shreveport."

Chief Laird said, "And that means Delta City doesn't have a police chief anymore."

Dan Arthur said, "Don't worry. I think I can keep things going until you select a new chief and get him appointed."

Chief Laird said, "Dan Arthur, I know you've always said that you didn't want to be anything but a patrol officer, but we'd like for you to rethink that. The mayor and I want you to take over as chief."

The mayor quickly said, "Look, Dan Arthur, you're the only officer on the force who'd be qualified for the chief's job. With all of the courses you've taken, having you riding in a patrol car is just a total waste of your talents."

Chief Laird added, "And if you don't take the job we'll have to hire somebody from outside Delta City who won't know the people here and won't know how our town works and won't know all the things Bigfoot taught you."

At the mention of Bigfoot's name, Dan Arthur felt a small twinge of guilt. Bigfoot had always put the people of Delta City first, so if he turned down the chief's job he would always feel like he had let down both his mentor and the people of Delta City.

Everyone was silent for a few moments, then Chief Laird said, "I didn't hear him say no, did you Mayor?"

The mayor said, "Nope. So what about it, Dan Arthur? Can we count on you?"

Dan Arthur smiled and said, "I don't want Bigfoot to come back and haunt me so I guess I'm in."

The mayor said, "Okay! If it's agreeable with you, the City Council would like to go ahead and get you sworn in today so you can get started." Taking Dan Arthur's arm, the mayor guided him toward the City Council chamber saying, "Come on, Chief Truman, you know the council doesn't like it when their meetings start late!"

CHAPTER 134

It was just before eleven o'clock on Halloween night, and the costume party at the University Club was in full swing.

The bartender, Mark Andrews, smiled as he surveyed the crowd.

Most of the patrons were students at Delta City University, and many of their costumes showed a fair amount of creativity. Of course, some of the costumes had obviously been residing on the shelves at Wal-Mart until a few hours earlier, and a few of the jocks simply put on a jersey bearing the number of their favorite sports figure and called that a costume. But great costume or not, everybody seemed to be having a good time.

A female voice called out, "Mark, can we get another round over here?" After checking to see who had yelled, Mark loaded a tray with a variety of drinks, along with a requisite margarita.

The tray's destination was a table presided over by a forty-something blonde woman wearing a princess costume. The other occupants of the table were some of the clubs regulars, who were more than happy to let the princess buy their booze.

As Mark passed out the drinks, he could hear the woman saying, "I love Halloween! One time me and my friends got dressed up like witches and cast some spells and killed my ex-husband, the bastard!"

Walking back toward the bar Mark thought, "*Well, I guess we're about five minutes away from her pulling her boobs out!*" and after placing the tray on the bar, he walked into the club's office and picked up the phone.

CHAPTER 135

Exclaiming, "Shit!" Dan Arthur Truman picked up his ringing cell phone from the bedside table and walked into the bathroom.

Closing the door, he spoke into the phone, saying, "Truman."

"Dan Arthur, It's Mark at the University Club. Nicole's out here talking about some kind of witchcraft shit, and I figure we're getting close to tit-flash time."

Dan Arthur replied, "Okay, Mark, thanks for calling. Cairn was over here so I could help her crate up some of her paintings to send to New Mexico, and she left here about an hour ago. She was going to swing by Mike's Restaurant and get something to eat, then come over and drive Nicole home. But if Nicole gets to be too much to handle before Cairn gets there, give me a call back and I'll send an officer by to pick her up."

"Will do. Thanks, Dan Arthur."

Dan Arthur hung up the phone and walked back into the bedroom, thinking, *"Bigfoot, you taught me well. I think I can safely say that I'm a damned good small town cop."*

As Dan Arthur replaced the cell phone on the nightstand the woman in the bed said, "Everything okay, Chief Truman?"

Climbing in beside her, Dan Arthur said, "Just Nicole out at the University Club. She's drunk and talking about that witchcraft thing again. Cairn should be there in a couple of minutes, but if Nicole starts getting out of hand before then Mark's going to call me back and I'll have one of my men take her home."

Taking his wife in his arms, Dan Arthur said, "Now where were we?" Barbara Mason Truman grinned and said, "You were just getting ready to stick your big old cop dick in me again, so get on with it!"

###

ABOUT THE AUTHOR

Bill Denton is a native of Raleigh, NC, who spent his formative years in Southeast Arkansas.

His first foray into suspense/horror/supernatural fiction came in the ninth grade with a short story titled *The Silence*. It was the tale of a young man trying to keep his fear in check as he makes his way across a graveyard on a dark night. He almost makes it, but trips and falls on a broken bottle. It closes with the line, "As the scarlet ribbon begins to flow the silence rules again." This earned him both an "A" and, needless to say, a trip to the guidance counselor's office.

Prior to embarking on his full-time writing career, Bill pursued a variety of occupations.

In high school he flipped hamburgers while playing drums in local rock and roll bands.

Following high school, Bill became a disc jockey, working at radio stations throughout the South and on the East Coast. He also honed his fiction writing skills by scripting radio advertisements.

As times changed in the radio industry disc jockeys were losing the freedom to be individually creative. So Bill shifted gears and began working as a designer/salesman in the civil engineering and fire protection industries. There he also wrote construction specifications, developing an ability to get to the point and tell it straight.

With the coming of personal computers, Bill again changed direction, becoming a programmer and one of the first Internet developers. While creating computer software and user manuals, he had the opportunity to work in a variety of styles in order to write instructions suited to a wide range of readers.

Through all of the twists and turns Bill's life has taken, he has always written. Short stories, songs (lyrics and music), whatever format best fit the demands of the particular muse he was satisfying.

Finally, Bill decided that writing full-time was the career he was destined for, and as he puts it, "I spent three years learning how to write a novel, and one year doing it."

The result was *Welcome to New Tipton*, Bill Denton's first novel. He also wrote a novella, *Fortune Cookies*, as a side project during the gestation period of *Welcome to New Tipton*.

Bill recently completed his second novel, *Surfer Girls*.

Bill believes that the greatest writing asset he has is all of the people who have passed through his life. "You take part of this person, part of that person, and put them in a story you have lived yourself or watched someone else live, and you can't help but end up with a compelling read."

In addition to writing, Bill continues to enjoy playing drums and guitar, and still plays with computers from time to time.

Bill now lives in Pittsburgh, PA. His family is rounded out by a son named Billy who shares his musical talents, and a miniature dachshund named Theodore, who shares his lunch.

Connect with me online

www.billdenton.com

www.ingramcontent.com/pod-product-compliance
Lightning Source LLC
Chambersburg PA
CBHW071129170626
46809CB00002B/542